DOUBLE CROSSED

By

Denise Hill

Double Crossed © 2014 by Denise Hill
ISBN-13: 978-0692400975
ISBN-10: 0692400974

Email address: dhpublishingco@gmail.com
Website: www.dhpublishingco.com

Cover Design: Kreative Solutions by Mahogani
Editing Service: Steve Soderquist

ACKNOWLEDGMENTS

I want to start out by thanking God for giving me the ability to write a second book. You have to understand that I never believed that I could publish my first book and since doing so, I feel more confident in myself to continue to do what I enjoy. Again, I want to thank my family and friends for their support and encouragement. I want to give thanks to my fans that supported my first novel. I really had fun with the characters in this book! I loved writing James and Lee I think this is one of my best novels. I hope you enjoy this as much as I enjoyed writing this novel.

Thank you and God bless!!!

Prologue

ЖЖ

Porsha walked further into Jerome's room, naked as the day she was born. With his back toward her, she snuck up behind him and wrapped her arms around his waist. Jerome stood still; he heard the sound of his door opening, but he hesitated to turn in the direction of the sound. He positioned himself with his gun ready to take out whoever was behind him when he felt arms wrapping around him. When he turned, he found Porsha standing there.

"Woman, what is wrong with you sneaking up on me like that?"

"I'm sorry..., did I scare you, sweetheart?"

Jerome looked at Porsha and shook his head.

"Jerome, I have missed you so much," she sighed.

Porsha stood on her tippy toes and kissed Jerome under his chin. She moved her way up and kissed him on his lips. Jerome moved his head and grabbed her by the arms, not allowing her to move. He bent his head down and circled her areola with his tongue before taking her nipple into his mouth.

Porsha removed her arms from his hold and removed the towel, exposing his body and the profused pole that she craved. Porsha moved down Jerome's body and stopped at his midsection, where she took her tongue and ran it across his head. She slid her tongue up and down the side of his penis before taking him into her mouth. Jerome stood, unable to move. The feeling was enough to curl his toes. He rolled his eyes back in his head as the feeling of Porsha's lips wrapped around him while her hands massaged his balls.

"Oh my God," Jerome groaned lightly.

Jerome found the strength to pull away from her and pulled her up. He grabbed her by her butt cheeks and lifted her off the floor. Porsha quickly spread her legs and wrapped them around his waist. He laid her down on the bed and buried his head between her legs, continuing to torture her until he couldn't take it anymore. He entered her with one hard thrust, moving in and out deeper and deeper until they both exploded with pleasure.

Chapter One

The Double Cross

"**Honey**, can you come up and zip me?" Natalie yelled down to her husband Jason, who was downstairs on the phone with one of his business partners,

"Yes, give me a minute!"

Jason climbed the stairs to where his wife awaited him.

Don't we look good tonight, Jason thought as he took in the way his wife looked in her short, black dress. He liked the way her toned golden brown thighs looked and the defined shape of her calves.

"Hey, let me call you a little later," Jason said on the phone as he continued to eye his wife as if she was a piece of cake.

"Damn you look good enough to eat, babe," Jason said as he moved further into the room. As he came closer, he observed how the black dress clung to her body, leaving no room to his imagination. Jason leaned down and started to kiss the nape of her neck, continuing down her back. He stopped at her rear end and moved his tongue upward against her spine, where the dress was open until he reached her neck. He cuffed her firm breast with his hands, allowing his finger to play with her nipples.

Natalie was so much in love with this man that even the smell of him turned her on. The thought of Jason's long, thick penis inside her began to drive her wild as she moved her ass against him. He slowly moved his hands down the side of her dress and slid it up. Jason turned her body around to face him before dropping to his knees. With one finger, he moved her thong to the side. Natalie parted her legs, giving him adequate room and with one swift movement, his tongue was teasing and taunting her womanhood. Natalie grabbed the back of his head, pulling him closer. The feel of his hot, thick tongue running up and down her caused her to lose her balance. Just as she began to fall, Jason caught her and laid her down softly on the carpet.

"Jason, please if you continue this we will never get out of here."

A ping of disappointment came over Jason's eyes; he knew that when he left tonight, he may never get another chance to spend with his wife if things didn't go as planned.

"You're right babe, we can finish this tonight."

"Is that a promise?" Natalie asked, looking up to him.
Jason smiled.

"You can bet your last dollar on it."
Natalie gazed down at her watch, "Jason, we need to leave now if we are going to make it before Lee arrives."
Jason asked one of Lee's friends, Ida, to take Lee out for a couple of drinks before the party. Jason and Natalie wanted time to get dressed without her questioning them, about tonight. Ida was supposed to entertain her until nine, then escort her to the party. Jason and Natalie have been planning a surprise birthday party for Lee's fifty- fifth birthday for months. The extravagant party began within an hour. Natalie wanted to be there before Lee arrived to make sure everything went as planned. Lee had played a huge role in their lives; this is one of the ways they want to show their appreciation by presenting her with a new Mercedes and a party to celebrate another year of them being together.
Natalie grabbed her mink coat and purse as the two rushed out the door. Walking to the car, Jason had a weird look on his face.

"Babe, what is going on?" Natalie asked her husband as he opened the passenger door for her.
Jason looked into her eyes.

"Nothing is wrong, babe. Stop worrying about nothing. Have I told you lately how much I love you?"
Natalie stopped in her tracks, staring into her husband's eyes. His behavior had been a little strange lately, she thought.
First, the threatening phone calls, and now Jason was acting as if this was their last time together.

"Why are you staring at me like that? You've been acting a little strange lately, not to mention the phone calls. I am beginning to worry, Jason."

"Sweetheart, how many times do I have to tell you that there's nothing for you to worry your pretty little self about? Haven't I always protected you?"

"Yes, you have sweetheart, but I feel as though things have...." she paused, looking up at him, "...gotten out of control. Your new clientele isn't like your normal clients. These people can be downright ruthless."

"Let me worry about them," Jason said confidently.

Cruising north on 465, the smooth sound of Donnell Jones blared through the speakers. Natalie peeked over at her husband. She couldn't help but admire the man sitting next to her. Not only was he handsome, but the love he had shown her over the years was something out of a fairy tale.

Natalie had given up everything to be with Jason, her family, and friends. He made a promise to her six years ago, that she would never want for anything and to this day, he has kept his promise.

The first two years of their marriage were a little shaky, but their relationship had since developed into something very special. Jason knew that giving up her family was hard for her, but she continued to be by his side. This showed him how much she loved and cared for him and because of that, he wanted their marriage to be worth it.

Natalie came from a religious family, with her father a Deacon in an apostolic church she grew up in. Her family was very strict, not allowing her to partake in any girly activities outside of the church. After graduating from college, her family still had a hold on her until she met the infamous Jason Jackson. Jason's bedroom eyes, his light brown complexion, and his bodacious body drew women to him from every race. Not to mention the way he treated women. This caused Natalie to fall- head-over-heels in love with him. Jason was known as a gangster to many… even through college. People referred to him and his friends as the black, 'Mafia'. They were college students by day and hustlers by night. Natalie's family was appalled when they learned that their only child was involved with such filth. Natalie had always been attracted to bad boys, but Jason was the first one she had ever brought home to meet her parents.

After dating for six months, Jason proposed to her. He asked her father for his blessing in their marriage. The answer did not come as a surprise to Natalie that her father rejected Jason's marriage proposal and forbidden Natalie from seeing Jason again. Without her parent's blessing and knowledge, Jason and Natalie eloped. Jason moved her from Merrillville to Indianapolis. Once they were married, the couple settled into their new home. Natalie tried several times to reach out to her parents, but they wanted nothing more to do with her for going against their wishes. The pain and sorrow that she bore over the years had not lessened, but she went on with her life as if she had not a care in the world… until now.

Focusing her attention back to her husband, Natalie became aware of a black van speeding along the passenger side. She couldn't see inside because the windows were tinted but her gut told her that trouble was ahead. When she glanced back at Jason, she spotted another car along the driver's side, but before Natalie had an opportunity to say anything, the car on the driver's side rammed the front- end of his car into theirs. They pulled out a shotgun and fired into their car several times, hitting Jason in the chest.

Jason lost control of the car, it spun out of control before slamming into the other car, causing both cars to burst into flames.

The next thing Natalie recalled or thinks she recalled, was her husband pulling her out of the burning car, but according to the detectives, this was impossible. Her husband's body was found in their car with two bullet wounds to his chest. The report said he died instantly.

Chapter Two

Things are not always, what they seem

As Natalie lay in the hospital bed with a concussion and a fractured ankle, she couldn't believe that her husband was dead. She knew he pulled her from the car, and she didn't really care what anyone thought.

"Derrick, I can't believe you agreed with the detectives that Jason is dead. He is not dead. He pulled me from the burning car. You have got to believe me."

Derrick just shook his head.

"Natalie, I believe you want to believe Jason is alive, but the evidence speaks for itself; Jason is dead. He died from the gunshot wounds, then burned in the fire," Derrick said softly as he wiped the tears from Natalie's face.

"How dare you say that!" Natalie, with eyes narrowed, yelled as she slapped Derrick's hand away. Derrick, who was Jason's longtime friend. He knew the kind of trouble they were facing. He knew the people they dealt with did not play. This was their message to let him know what happened to people who tried to double- cross them. Now, his only worries were how to keep himself out of harm's way in order to be there for Natalie.

A month ago to this day, Jason made Derrick promise to look after Natalie if anything should ever happen to him. Now, the time had come for him to keep his promise to his friend.

Lee, Jason's long time live in housekeeper has been at Natalie's side the entire time. Lee took care of all the burial arrangements and made sure Natalie wanted for nothing. After being in the hospital for several days, it was time for Natalie to bury the man she loved more than life.

The funeral was larger than Natalie expected. She was surprised to see so many men from the police force in attendance. Did they know my husband, she wondered? Why are they here? At the gravesite behind the church, Natalie noticed eight men dressed in black suits that stayed away from the other attendants. It almost seemed as if they were there to bear witness that Jason was truly dead. Natalie speculated they were the reason she had to lay her loved one to rest. There were many questions running through her head and no answers to any of them. Someone had to know something, and if it was the last thing that she did, she would find out who murdered her husband. The eight men at the funeral never came up to Natalie to give her their condolences and never mingled with any other people in attendance. The police, on the other hand, all came over to her and told her how sorry they were to learn that her husband had been murdered. They told her that they would do whatever it took to catch his killer.

With everything happening so fast, she completely forgot about calling her parents, but she knew they would probably refuse to speak to her, as they had done in the past. She was thankful that she had Lee and Derrick at her side.

The ride home from the gravesite was quiet. Thoughts of who murdered her husband continued to run through her mind. Why would someone want to do this to Jason, she wondered?
As the town car pulled into the driveway, Natalie had a feeling of emptiness. As she stepped out of the car with Derrick and Lee at her side, she looked sorrowfully around at the home she shared with her husband.
The three-story brick home didn't seem like home anymore. It was ugly, cold, and haunted her as she stared. The warmness that always greeted her… was no longer there. As she moved up the walkway, she felt Jason all around her. She could sense his smell in the air. Could this be because she had just buried and say goodbye to him? Natalie felt his aura so strong around her. She would give anything to be able to see him one more time.
Derrick led Natalie inside the house. She glanced up at the staircase and groaned.
    "Don't worry, I'll carry you up," Derrick said gently.
Derrick puts his arm around her waist and slightly bent down to place his other arm underneath her legs. He made his way upstairs to Natalie's room. He placed her gently on her bed and removed her shoe.

"Oh my God, this boot is so uncomfortable," Natalie whined and groaned.

"It'll take you some time getting used to wearing it," Derrick said softly.

"I'll send Lee up to help you get undressed. Would you like for me to do anything before I head downstairs?" Derrick asked as he looked at Natalie with lust in his eyes.

"No, I am good, thanks." She said trying to hold back the tears that have been threatening to fall.

Derrick headed for the door, stopped and turned back to Natalie.

… "Oh, by the way, some of the people from Lee's church stopped by earlier and dropped off plenty of food. Let Lee or I know when you are ready to eat."

She looked up, her eyes soft. "Derrick, thank you for all you have done. Please make yourself at home, and feel free to stay in one of the guest rooms for as long as you like."

"Thanks," Derrick said with the biggest grin on his face.

Seeing his smile made her miss Jason even more.

"Derrick, I can't believe Jason is gone," she said as the tears that she tried to hold back began to fall. Derrick rushed to her side to comfort her. He wiped away her tears with his fingers and took a seat on the bed beside her.

"Natalie… sweetheart, I know, I can't believe he's gone either, but you know Jason wouldn't want you to mourn over him like this. He loved you so much and made sure that you were taken care of. He would want you to move on with your life." A ping of guilt hit Derrick. He thought to himself. What am I thinking telling her not to mourn her husband's death? Derrick left Natalie's room and closed the door behind him. He leaned against the door; guilt and remorse flooding his thoughts. How could he live with himself, how could he tell the woman that he had been in love with all these years, that it was he that had set her husband up? When Derrick introduced Jason to Rico the kingpin. He knew what Jason's intentions were and evidently, told Rico. Jason's dad had been Rico's dad's right - hand man in the big drug --world, but when Jason's dad wanted to retire to spend more time with his family, Rico's dad had him killed. Jason vowed if it was the last thing that he did, he would take down the Lorenz family. So when Derrick told Rico this, he had his men murder him, which left room for Derrick to be with Natalie. Derrick walked down the hall to the guest room, where he will remain until he won Natalie's, heart

Lee knocked at Natalie's door before entering. She brought Natalie water to take with her pain pills the doctor prescribed for her.
She smiled a little.
"How are you doing?"
"I'm not doing so good Ms. Lee. I wish I could have seen this coming. I should have done something when Jason started getting those threatening phone calls." Natalie sobbed.
Lee hugged her. "Honey, what could you have done?"
"I don't know, but I feel like I should have done something… like, go to the police."
"Jason was a grown man, he knew what he was doing and he knew the consequences." She nodded
"If he knew what he was doing, then why isn't he here with me now!" Natalie shouted.
"Natalie, let me tell you what my mother always told me. Things happen for a reason. Nothing happens that God does not allow. We may not know right at this moment, why, but later you will see." With her own very heavy heart, Lee continued to sit at Natalie's side until she fell asleep. She still couldn't believe Jason was gone. He was her only son; a secret she kept from everyone in order to keep herself, safe. Jason made her promise never to expose their identity.
After a while, Lee made her way back to her suite where she broke down. The tears that she held inside in order to be strong for Natalie poured out uncontrollably. Unfortunately, there's no one there to help her through her pain and comfort her.
Lee sees her life changing for the worse if only she could reach out to her sister, but in doing so would only have others uncover her and Jason's secret.

Natalie woke from her dream. She ran her hand across her lips, but the rocking of the chair caught her attention. She watched the chair slowly rock back and forth as if someone had been sitting there. She looked around the spacious room as if she was looking for someone. She stared at the hidden closet that was hidden behind the fireplace mantel. She looked over at the white chaise, where Jason's sweatpants and tee shirt were laying. She glanced at his shoes as they sat on the other side of the chaise. Natalie felt Jason's presence everywhere.

"It was a dream wasn't it?" She asked herself, "it felt so real," she said out loud. She had dreamed that Jason had come to her and told her that things are not always what they seemed and that they would be together again…, and then he kissed her goodbye. Natalie continued to sit up in bed as she thought about her dream of Jason. Natalie missed him even more. Her heart ached for him. Now she wondered if Jason knew what lay ahead for him. She remembered the way he acted their last night together.

Later that afternoon, Derrick walked down to the kitchen where he found Lee preparing a tray of food to take to Natalie.

"Where are you going with that tray," Derrick asked as he looked at Lee with so much hatred.

"I'm taking Natalie some dinner," Lee said as she looked back at him with just as much hate in her eyes.

"Why don't you set the table for Natalie and me? I'll go and bring her down for dinner."
He looked at her. "Lee, things will be different around here now that Jason is gone. You might not want to hang around anymore," Derrick said touching Lee's hand.

"What do you mean?"
Lee asked as she jerked her hand away from Derrick. The blood in her veins had started to boil. She hated this man more each day.
He looked at her, chuckling. "You know what I mean. You and I have never really gotten along with each other; if you want to stay in this house, things will have to change between us."
Lee glared at Derrick with hatred.

"Derrick, it doesn't matter that we don't we get along or even like each other. The one thing that we have in common is Natalie."
Derrick glared.

"I am not here for you and you are not here for me. We are both here for her, so let's not forget that. When I am ready to leave, I will leave… but not until I decide it, not you."
Derrick looked at Lee and mumbled under his breath.

"No, you will leave when I tell you to, you old bitch."

18

Even though Lee did not look a day over 40 and had a body that most young women would die for, Derrick continued to call her old… but at one time he had a little crush on her, but since Lee disliked him so much and caused problems for Derrick with Jason, his crush had turned into hate.

Chapter Three

Showing your true colors

After Lee prepared the table, she headed down the hall to her room. To see Derrick walking around as if he was the man of the house brought tears to her eyes. Lee cried not only for herself but for Natalie as well. She had no idea what type of man Derrick was and the danger he could put her in. Lee vowed to keep Natalie out of harm's way, but Derrick was a ruthless man who will go to any means to get whatever he wanted. She knew Derrick wanted Natalie. She had told Jason this on several occasions, but he refused to listen. Just like his dad, he trusted people a little too much. Lee loved Natalie as if she were her own daughter, and would do anything to keep her out of the arms of someone like Derrick, even if it killed her.

"Why isn't Lee having dinner with us? I'm accustomed to the three of us having dinner…" Natalie stopped and looked up, "I'm sorry Derrick. I'm speaking as if Jason was still here."

"No apology necessary…, but Natalie, you have to face the fact that Jason is gone, and that he will not be coming back. The sooner you realize this, the better things will be for you." He had harshness leaking from his voice.

Natalie couldn't help but feel a little irritated and angry with Derrick. His tone was more demanding than sympathy.

"If you'll excuse me," Natalie said curtly. "I want to check on Lee."

"Natalie! Lee is a big girl. She can take care of herself."

Natalie looked back at Derrick with a look on her face that said nigga, have you lost your damn mind yelling at me like that.

"I know Lee is a big girl, but what you fail to realize is that Jason was like a son to her for many years, this has to be hard on her as well."

Derrick shook his head as Natalie struggled to remove herself from the table.

"This is not going to be easy," he said under his breath. "Lee has to go." He had to figure out a way to make Natalie see she didn't need her around anymore.

Natalie grabbed a hold of her crutches and slowly made her way down the hall to Lee's room. As she approached the door, she stood there a minute before knocking. She turned to her right and looked at the top of the stairs and pictured Jason standing there… as she has done so many times, but this time Jason was not standing there looking down at her. Natalie turned back to the door and knocked a couple of times at Lee's door before she opened.

"Are you okay Ms. Lee?

"Yes, Natalie… I'm fine. How are you holding up?'

Natalie could tell that Ms. Lee had been crying.

"Ms. Lee, I know Jason was like a son to you, so I know you're hurting just as I am."

Struggling with her crutches, Natalie walked further into the room and sat down beside Lee, placed her arms around her.

"Oh Natalie, I miss him so much, but I'm trying to be strong for you because I know this is what Jason would have wanted me to do… but it's so hard." Natalie began to shed her own tears for Jason.

"I don't know what I am going to do without him. He was my life and with him gone, I feel no need to go on." Natalie looked up and stared at the ceiling shaking her head.

"Natalie, don't you talk like that. Jason wouldn't want you to feel this way. Jason would want you to go on with your life and to enjoy every bit of it." She shook her head. "I don't know Ms. Lee," Natalie said as she wiped the tears from her face. "I feel so weak and helpless. I feel as though Jason isn't dead." She looked directly into her eyes.

"In fact, I know he isn't dead. He pulled me from the burning car, but people continue to tell me that that's impossible. What do you think?"

Natalie looked at her. "How can you be so sure that it was Jason that pulled you from the car and not someone else?"

Natalie laughed.

"Trust me, I know my husband, and I know what he looks like…, if I don't know anything else, I know that much. I know the feel of his touch and the way he smells, I know he pulled me from the car and it's driving me crazy that no one believes me."Ms. Lee grabbed

Natalie's hand and looked at her with a serious face. "Do me a favor and keep that bit of information to yourself. I don't want anyone thinking that you are losing it and place you into one of those crazy homes. Jason would roll over in his grave if he knew I allowed that to happen."

Lee wanted so badly to tell Natalie about Derrick. She wanted to warn her not to trust him…, but right now, she knew this was not the right time to address her concerns and decided to keep it to herself.

Back in the dining room, Derrick sat at the kitchen table furiously. He wanted to spend time with Natalie, but all she wanted to do was to comfort that nosy old bitch. She was the one who needed comforting and that is where he came in. "Doesn't she know how long I have waited to wrap my arms around her and to feel her body against mine?" He thought to himself.

Just then, Derrick felt a pain of remorse soar through his body. He knew that if Jason's friends knew he was behind the setup, and that he was trying to move in on Natalie, his body would be discovered in the White River, or somewhere. He knew he would have to be careful and play his cards just right in order for Natalie and him to be together without anyone becoming suspicious.

For years, he had wanted Natalie for himself. He had many dreams where Natalie came running into his arms. Now he saw his dreams as a reality. He would not let anyone or anything stand in his way, not even Lee.

Later that night as Natalie lay in bed and dozed off, she awoke as she felt someone's lips on hers. She opened her eyes and immediately jumped and was disgusted when she sees Derrick.

"Derrick, what the hell are you doing?" Natalie yelled.

"Calm down Natalie, I just came to kiss you goodnight and to see if you needed anything before I turned in."

"No, I'm fine," Natalie replied as she pulled the covers up to her chest. "Get Out."

"Okay, okay," Derrick said as he started out of the room, then turned back around.

"Good night Nat."

An uneasy feeling came over Natalie as Derrick left her room. From now on, I will have to make sure I lock my door," Natalie told herself as she grabbed her crutches and made her way to lock the door.

Chapter Four

A gut feeling

Down the hall, Derrick stood glancing out of the guest bedroom window.

"This is not going as planned," he mumbled to himself.

Derrick continued to stare out the window, lost in his thoughts when a pair of headlights caught his attention. He noticed a car speeding off. It was the same car that was parked outside of the home when they returned from Jason's funeral. He started to wonder if Rico and his men were on to him.

The next morning, Derrick walked outside to grab the newspaper and noticed the same black car parked down the street. He had a good mind to approach the car to see if the driver was inside, but had second thoughts. Derrick made his way back inside the house where Lee greeted him.

"Good morning Derrick," Lee said as she glided down the stairs.

"I was on my way out to get the paper, but I see you've gotten it already."

Lee was trying to do her best not to show Derrick her dislike and distrust in him.

"Do you happen to know who owns the Black Viper Park down the street?" Derrick asked.

Lee glanced out the window to get a better view of the car in question.

"No…, this is the first time I've seen the car. Why, are you worried about something?"

"No, why would I?" He looked uncomfortable.

"You seem to be worried about a car parked down the street. Most people could care less about a parked car unless they have something to hide or if they are worried about something"

"What are you trying to say, Lee?"

"I'm not trying to say anything."

Derrick despised Lee more each day. She had no idea that he was trying to find a way to get rid of her. She was the only thing keeping Natalie and him apart. Derrick walked down the hall to the kitchen.

"I could have sworn I smelled bacon, eggs, and coffee this morning," Derrick said aloud.

Lee continued to do what she had to do and ignored Derrick's comment. Little did he know she had already prepared breakfast for Natalie and herself. Natalie and Lee had been up for hours talking and had breakfast out back on the deck. Lee looked back at Derrick. I will be damned if I make breakfast for that motherfucker. Who does he think he is walking around here as if he owns this place? If Jason were here, he would kick his ass every time he got a chance for trying to move in on Natalie. Lee thought, before being interrupted.

"Is breakfast going to be served this morning?" Derrick asked.

"Sure, if you want to make it yourself," Lee replied with a grin.

Lee continued with her morning chores, trying so hard not to laugh at the dumb expression on Derrick's face.

"You are such a loser… who in their right mind would want you, looking like Mike Tyson and Fifty- cent rolled into one," Lee said under her breath.

Natalie showered, dressed, and made her way downstairs using her crutches. She was still afraid to put any pressure on her ankle so she continued to use her crutches, but trying to come down the stairs was proving to be difficult for her.

"This is harder than I thought," Natalie said as she missed a step and almost tumbled down the stairs until Derrick caught her.

"Natalie, I thought I told you to let me know when you were ready to come down."

"I know, but I wanted to try this on my own. What will I do when you and Lee aren't here?"

"Well, you won't have to worry about that because I will never leave your side."

"Don't you have a job to go to?" Lee asked."

"Yes, my job is to take care of Natalie. What's your job?"

She eyed him angrily.

"To take care of Jason's home and his wife; or have you forgotten that already?"

Natalie could tell that there was bad- blood between the two. She had always been aware of Ms. Lee's dislike in Derrick, but she had never witnessed Derrick's dislike in her.

Lee stood back and watched the interaction between Natalie and Derrick; she knew what Derrick's intentions were.

"If only James and John were here," Lee whispered.

James and John had been friends with Jason since elementary school. She considered them true friends, unlike Derrick, but since their disappearance, things had gone downhill.

Lee would swear on a stack of bibles that Derrick had something to do with their disappearance... unable to prove it, her suspicions had mounted and added to the rift between them.

Natalie looked up in time to see the look of hate that Lee displayed as she watched Derrick help her from the stairs. Natalie watched; her thoughts guarded.

"I need Derrick in my life right now; Ms. Lee will just have to understand."

Chapter Five

Meeting of the minds

Two months later

He parked outside the home every night since Natalie returned home from the hospital, but what he couldn't understand is why Derrick was still hanging around. It had been two months since the accident; Natalie no longer needed help, and if she did, Lee was there to help her.

He looked at his watch; it was five minutes till nine. He had five minutes to make it to the warehouse for his meeting with James and John.

"Derrick, I'll deal with you later." He said as he drove off. Derrick, who was in the house crouching down in front of the window, watched as the black sports car drove off. Now, he was anxious. He was not sure who the driver was, but he knew it had to be Rico or his men. Rico and his men were responsible for Jason's death… and now he felt as if he was next on their list.

What Derrick didn't know was Rico had a few other officers on his payroll who kept him informed about the undercover investigations that were going on against him and his family. He also knew that Derrick was a dirty cop working undercover.

Jason met Derrick eight years ago. Derrick was dirty, then, but over the years, he had become consumed with greed. Jason thought Derrick was a straight up guy until three weeks before his death when an undercover agent informed Jason that Derrick had snitched on him, but what Derrick failed to realize is what goes around; comes back around in due time.

John and James watched as the Viper pulled onto the lot. They both eyed the tall, broad shoulders of the man emerging from the car.

"Check him out," John said to James.

"I see him." James nodded. "He just had to bring her out."

"It's about time you showed up! I thought I was going to have to come and find you," John said jokingly.

"I'm sorry, but I have a few things to take care of and since the two of you have no life anymore, I knew it wouldn't be a problem if I ran late." He said sarcastically.

"Should I guess where you were," James said, looking at him."

"How is she doing?" James asked.

Jerome replied as he smiled. "I would say pretty well for someone who's just lost the love of her life."

James decided to change the subject. "We have a lot of work ahead of us, so let's get down to business."

Jerome tossed a folder on the desk.

"Here's all information on Rico's men. He has a few of our own on his payroll. Ralph, Carl, Johnny, and Paul are all on Rico's payroll. Rico and his men are getting suspicious of Ricky, so we'll l have to remove him for his safety."

"If we remove him, how will we know what's going on," James asked.

"That's what we're going to have to figure out. We'll need to know when the deal is going down. We'll also need someone on the inside, but I don't want to risk Ricky's life by keeping him in. We need a woman to get close to Rico. You know how he is when it comes to his women; he will lose all control, and this is what we will be counting on.

"Leave that to me," John said, I have the perfect person for this job. She will be our eyes and ears on the inside."

"We'll also have to watch our backs with our own. We don't know how much they know about the accident. Right now, we can't trust anyone."

"I've been checking out Rico's crib for several weeks now. He travels with two of his men everywhere he goes and he leaves the other six at home. I have got to find a way to get in there without being detected by the surveillance cameras."

John nodded. "I think that's going to be a problem… besides, it's too dangerous. We need someone on the inside. I'll handle that."

"Who do you have in mind?" James asked.

John smiled. "Wouldn't you like to know," he said.

Jerome looked at John suspiciously, "I am not even going there."

"When will you contact her?"

"It's already done."

"I have a new location where you guys can hide out; somewhere where you'll be more comfortable and it's more secluded."
Jerome tossed a set of keys to John. It was the keys to his cabin in Gatlinburg.

"Can I have my contact come down to the cabin?"

"Yes, that's cool."

"Have you had any contact with Lee?" James asked.

"No... I haven't, I'm waiting for the right time to reach out to her," Jerome said as he walked over to the window and looked out at the empty parking lot. "You guys should head toward the cabin tonight or first thing in the morning. Contact me once you get there. I'll probably head your way in a couple weeks. Until then, please stay out of sight."

"And you be careful," James said as he pats Jerome on the shoulder.
Jerome gave John a nod; an unspoken gesture.
The men left the warehouse, heading in different directions. Jerome drove forty-five miles from the city where he had a condo that no one knew about. He purchased the condo years ago and kept it a secret from the world. He knew that when you work undercover you couldn't really trust anyone ---not even your best friends.
Jerome trusted James and John with his life, but he had never told them about this place. He did some things there, they would not be happy about. This was the place where he fell in love with a married woman. This was their getaway. This was where he was the happiest and felt free from the world of trouble. After the affair ended, Jerome would come here when he wanted to reminisce about the love he couldn't have.
Jerome pulled onto the interstate. He put his Musiq- Soulchild CD in and listened as he drove to his condo. Jerome moved his head to the beat as he thought about Derrick and what he did to Jason. Now, he was living in the home of the man he snitched on with his wife. This was eating Jerome up inside. He wanted badly to kill Derrick, but if he did, he would be no better than Rico.

Forty- five minutes later, Jerome pulled into his driveway his mind returning to the present as he turned off the ignition, got out of the car and headed toward the door. As he put the key in the lock, he noticed a postcard that had fallen to the ground. When he picked it up, he noticed a familiar address.

"It can't be," he said out loud.

Jerome made his way inside his condo. He removed his jacket and turned on the living room light. He looked at the postcard more carefully. When he turned it over, Jerome reads:

"Jay, I love and miss you very much, Porsha."

Feelings of love and lust that he didn't know still existed arose in him. He couldn't believe she had the nerve to try and reach out to him. It had been over six years since he had last seen or spoken to her. Things did not end well between the two. After leaving her that night, he had made a promise that he would never have anything to do with her again. She had broken his heart.

She made him do things that he had never done with or for any woman in his lifetime. Jerome now considered Porsha to be a poisonous snake once she released her venom; it was all over for... a brother. It took Jerome a long time to get her out of his system.

Jerome tossed the postcard onto the table and headed for his bedroom. He kicked off his shoes, removed his pants and headed for the shower where a vision of Porsha clouded his mind. He remembered all the times they made love in the shower, and later in the hallway. They were so hot for each other that they couldn't make it to the bedroom. There were so many good times he shared with Porsha here. Jerome stood under the shower with both hands against the wall as the water ran down his body. Just the thought of Porsha stirred feelings in his groin.

"Damn, this can't be happening." He said out loud. Jerome continued to stand under the shower as the water became cold, which brought his mind back to the present.

Jerome shuts off the water and grabbed his towel and was headed to his bedroom where he dried off and hopped in his bed butt- naked. Jerome propped his pillows up and laid back with both hands behind his head. His thoughts were of Porsha. He wondered after six years, why all of a sudden she would reach out to him. Out of all people to contact him, it had to be her. Someone he vowed to have nothing to do with.

Chapter Six

The shit hits the fan

The next morning Derrick's cell rings, waking him out of his sleep. He looked at the clock it was eight in the morning. He wiped the sleep from his eyes.

"Who in the hell could be calling me this early." He rolled over... grumbling.

Derrick grabbed his cell phone from the nightstand and glanced at the number.

"Oh, shit!" If I don't answer then Rico will think something is up. Does he know about me?"

All these thoughts ran through Derrick's head before answering the phone.

"Hello?"

"What's up Derrick? Where have you been hiding?"

Derrick closed his eyes.

"Hey Rico, you know I haven't been hiding anywhere. I thought it would be a good thing to lay low for a while."

"That was a good idea, but it's been two months since Jason's death. I don't think anyone has suspected you as being a rat. I need to meet with you today to talk about some issues that have come up."

"What issues," Derrick asked, his guard up now?

"Just meet me at the coffee shop on 56th and Emerson at noon and I'll fill you in on the details."

Derrick's eyes were still closed. "Alright, I'll be there."

After hanging up with Rico, Derrick laid there with his mind full of thoughts. What was going on now? He wondered. He did everything that Rico asked, so what could be the problem?

Rico arrived at noon. Derrick had arrived thirty minutes early to check out the spot. For some reason, he didn't feel good about today's meeting. He wanted to make sure he was not being set up. When

Derrick arrived, he went inside the coffee shop. He looked around before heading to the men's restroom to make sure no one was hiding inside. Once the coast was clear, Derrick positioned himself in the corner of the coffee shop where he could see who came in and left out.

Derrick was sitting at the table waiting nervously when Rico and two of his men arrived.

"Hey, Derrick... how's it going?"

Derrick could tell something wasn't right by the tone of Rico's voice.

"What's up?" Derrick said, eyeing him.

"I thought you would tell me," Rico said as he took his seat in front of Derrick eyeing him suspiciously.

"What are you talking about, Rico?" Derrick asked as he stared straight at Rico with his heart beating rapidly.

"Derrick, do you take me for a fool?"

"Man, what are you talking about?" Derrick lit a cigarette watching him carefully.

"The money Derrick... where's my money?" Rico yelled angrily as he hit his fist on the table. The few people in the coffee shop turned to look in their direction.

"What money are you talking about?"

"Oh, so now you have amnesia. How about we take a ride and see if your memory comes back?" Rico's men grabbed Derrick as he tried to jerk away from them, but being that they were much stronger than he was, they won the battle drug him outside to Rico's car.

The few customers and workers that were inside the restaurant, looked away; to keep from being a witness to anything.

"Rico, I have no idea what you're talking about," Derrick said as the men pushed him into the back seat of Rico's car.

Rico entered the car from the other side while the two men position themselves in the front seat.

"Drive around for a while," Rico said as he pointed a silencer to Derrick's head.

"Come on Rico man... what the hell is going on? I did what you asked me to do, so what's the problem?"

"The problem is, you cheated me out of $1 million dollars, that's the problem," Rico said trying to control his anger.

"What are you talking about...? I cheated you out of $1 million?"

"The money that you were supposed to take to Charlie's the night before Jason's murder. It was $1 million short."

Derrick was shaking his head now. "That's impossible. I counted the money before we left and it was all there."

Rico just looked at him. "Well, maybe you can't count because Charlie called me right after the two of you left accusing me of trying to rip him off. Do you know how that makes me look to people? I may be many things, but a crook ain't one of them."

Derrick was actually afraid. "Rico, there has got to be an explanation as to why the money was not there.

I swear to you that when I counted the money, it was all there. Maybe Jason stole the money without me knowing it."

"Well, we can't ask him now can we?"

Rico demanded Derrick turn and face him. He pointed the silencer to Derrick's forehead.

"I am tired of playing with your ass, now… where is my fucking money? I let you walk around here for two months while I took care of other business arrangements out of state, but now it's time to pay up, or you will end up like your friend Jason. I don't know how you're going to come up with the million dollars, but I better have my money in two weeks… if not, you know the deal." Rico demanded the car to be stopped.

"Lonnie, take this mother-fucker back to his car before I blow his brains out."

Derrick sat in his car, sweat pouring out of him like a waterfall. He knew the money was all there when he handed the briefcase over to one of Charlie's men. He replayed the scene repeatedly in his head, and then it dawned on him. He left Jason alone with the briefcase case for a short period of time when he stopped off to see Regina. As Derrick turned the corner onto Natalie's Street, he noticed the Viper parked two houses down from Natalie's home. Derrick pulled up behind the car and sat there for a minute before getting out of his own car. He walked around the car before peering into the driver's window. The windows were tinted, which prevented him from seeing anything.

Jerome sat there amused as he watched Derrick, "this dumb asshole. The windows are tinted! They are tinted for a reason. I should blow my horn just to scare the hell out of him…. Fucking idiot."

Chapter Seven

Enough is enough

Derrick rushed into the house yelling, "Natalie, where are you?" Lee stepped out of her room to see what all the commotion was.

"What's going on," Lee asked?

"Mind your own business, old woman," he growled. Natalie walked out of her room into the hallway in time to hear Derrick's remark to Lee.

"Derrick, what's come over you? Why would you speak to Ms. Lee that way?"

His eyes narrowed. "She needs to mind her own fucking business," Derrick said angrily as he pushed Natalie back into her room, closing the door. He stepped inside for a moment. He grabbed hold of her arm.

"Natalie, I need for you to listen and to listen carefully. Did Jason say anything to you about money he stole from Rico?" Her eyes widened. "What? What are you talking about? You know damn well Jason didn't have to steal money from anyone."

"Natalie shut the fuck up and listen!" Derrick yelled as he shoved Natalie to the bed.

"I need to know where the safe is in the house and I need to know... now." After hearing the commotion, Lee climbed the stairs to Natalie's room and walked in with her 38 in hand, right as Derrick raised his hand to strike Natalie. Lee saw what was going on and took action.

"Don't you dare put your hands on her you son of a bitch," Lee grumbled ready to take Derrick out if needed. Derrick turned around to see Lee standing with her gun. He stepped away from Natalie and took a seat in the chair.

"I am so sorry. I don't know what came over me. Lee walked over to Natalie and sat next to her on the bed. She looked at Natalie and then at Derrick.

"I think it is time for you to leave," Lee said furiously.

Derrick jumped up from the chair. He knew he had to come up with an excuse to stay in order to find the safe.

"I can't. Natalie's life is in danger because of Jason."

"What are you talking about?" Lee asked.

"Jason stole money from a drug dealer and if I don't come up with it, I am dead." He paused. "I mean, Natalie's dead."

"What does this have to do with me? I don't even know these people; I have never laid eyes on any of them."

"It doesn't matter, Natalie. Jason stole from them, and they want their money… or someone will pay for it."

"Why would Jason do this?" Natalie asked.

"I can't answer that. I know the money was there when Jason and I left Rico's the day before his death."

"Oh, so you told them that Jason stole the money," Lee said carefully, eyeing him.
Lee didn't waiver.

"He had to have taken it because I didn't. I counted the money myself, so I know how much was there."

"You are such a fucking loser." Her gun raised. "You blame a dead man for stealing money from a drug dealer. How can you stoop so low, Derrick? I knew you were not to be trusted, but to lie on a dead man, really, who does that?" Derrick was now looking down at the end of a 38 and was petrified, more so, from the fact, the weapon didn't waver an inch.

"Lee, I know you don't want to think Jason would do something like this, but you didn't know Jason like I did."
She eyed him hard. "Please, I knew Jason better than you think. To be honest, I think you had something to do with his death."

"Shut your mouth you old bitch, you don't know anything."
Lee rose up to face Derrick, her gun still aimed. "Go ahead and hit me, make my mother fucking day."

"Stop it," Natalie yelled. I can't take any more of this nonsense.

"I want the both of you to leave. I need some time alone."
Lee looked at Natalie. "Is this what you want? You want me to leave?"
Natalie was shaking slightly. "Yes, I think you need some time alone as well. Lee, I want you to do the things that you always wanted to do, but just never got around to do it… like visiting your sister in Ohio.

Shocked by Natalie's gesture, Lee headed for her room. Lee walked from the room and downstairs with her head held down. When she entered her room, she took a seat on the side of her bed and shook her head. She could not believe she was being asked to leave the home that she shared with her son for over six years.

Lee eased off the bed and made her way over to her closet where she found her luggage she received one Christmas from Natalie.

"I guess this gift did come in handy." She said softly as she pulled it out of her closet and laid it on her bed. Lee began to pack some of her belongings.

I can't believe she was asking me to leave after all I have done for her, Lee thought to herself. As she continued to pack, she heard a knock at the door. It was Natalie.

"Lee, I know you don't understand why I am asking you to leave, but in time, I will explain it to you. I want you to know that I love you very much, and your safety is my only concern at this moment." Lee opened the door and looked at her. "What about your safety Natalie?" Natalie's eyes had tears, "I will be fine, trust me." Natalie gave Lee a hug and a kissed her on the cheek.

"I will let you know when it is safe for you to return." Lee hugged her tighter. "Okay, I hope you know what you're doing."

After watching Lee drive off, Natalie felt guilty about not telling Lee what was really going on. She knew if she explained to Lee that John had phoned her late last night, Lee would refuse to leave Natalie alone with Derrick hanging around. John had a bad feeling in his gut, so he reached out to Natalie for her own safety to warn her about Derrick. He suggested that she should find a way to give Lee some time off to keep her safe. It wasn't a secret to any of them how much Derrick despised Lee. With Jason gone, no one could protect her from him.

Natalie agreed to help and try to get as much information out of Derrick as possible and report this information to John.

Lately, Natalie had been feeling a little uncomfortable with Derrick around. She noticed that he never spoke of Jason and seemed to get irritated when she brought his name up. This puzzled her until her phone call from John. Now she believed Derrick had something to do with her husband's murder.

"What the hell is going on," Jerome said, as he watched Lee drive off. He turned on the ignition and followed behind her. He stayed his distance so that she didn't notice his car. He was well aware that his car had been the focus of the conversation between Derrick and Lee. What no one knew was that Jerome was inside the home while the three attended Jason's funeral and placed little tiny microphones in each room. He could hear every conversation that went on and right now, he was not too happy with Natalie's behavior and the fact that she had asked Lee to leave nor was he happy about the closeness between Natalie and Derrick. He was definitely not happy about what transpired an hour ago inside the home. He was so close to running into the house and beating Derrick's ass, but he knew this would ruin everything.

Jerome continued to follow Lee as she pulled into the gas station. Lee went inside to get gas, snacks and to fill up her tank before her road trip to the cabin.

The cabin was Lee's favorite getaway; the seclusion and serenity was just what she needed at this point in her life.

After filling up her tank, Lee hopped onto the interstate, and took I-74; Jerome knew exactly where Lee was heading.

Chapter Eight

A surprise guest

Jerome pressed the OnStar button in his car, "Call James." The phone dialed James's number.

"Hey, Jerome what's up?"

"Hey, I wanted to give you a heads up; Lee is on her way to the cabin."

"How far is she?"

"She should be there in six hours or so."

"Did you tell her to come?"

"Now why would I do that? Natalie asked her to leave and take some time off. I know the cabin has always been her favorite place to go to get away from the world."

"And how is it that you know this information?"
Jerome laughed, "I have my way of knowing everything."
Jerome could almost see James shaking his head on the other end.

"Yeah, whatever you say." Jerome burst out laughing. "I will phone you once she hits the premise… later," Jerome clicked off.
Jerome turned on the recorder that translated all the conversations in Jason and Natalie's home as he continued to follow Lee.

Derrick sat in the guest room, scheming. He knew Jason had to have taken the money, but where would he put it? He wondered when he heard a knock at the door.
Natalie walked in, "You are still here I see."

"Yes, Natalie, I'm sorry for the way I acted earlier. I don't know what I am going to do or how I can protect you if I don't find the money."

"Why am I involved? Natalie asked as she made her way into the room and took a seat in the chair directly across from the bed Derrick was sitting on. "I had nothing to do with Jason or your dealings with these people. I feel as though you've involved me and I don't like it one bit."

"I would never do anything like that. You should know me better than that."

"Should I? The man that shoved me to the bed and was about to strike me?"

"That wasn't me, I wasn't myself back there."

"Who the hell was it then? You know right now you sound really stupid talking about how it wasn't you. Well, whoever it was, he better not try anything else with me if he knows what's good for him."

After the phone call from Jerome, James told John that Lee was heading to the cabin.

"I'm not surprised. I called Natalie last night and informed her about Derrick. She has agreed to help us get as much information out of him as possible. I also told her to get Lee out of the house for her safety. You know the two of them hate each other."

"You did what? Does Jerome know that you did this?"

"No, not yet."

"I hope you know what you just did. What if Natalie slips up and tells him about us?"

"Don't worry, she won't."

"Let's hope so for your sake. I would hate to be in your shoes if this backfires."

"Natalie can handle it. She's already had her own suspicion about Derrick."

"Did you tell her everything?"

"Come on now, I am not stupid."

"That remains to be in question," James said as he giggled. Johns gave him an evil look as he walked into the bathroom.

Later that evening Jerome phoned James. "She is in the proximity of the cabin. Make sure you knuckleheads don't fuck up our plan."

"There something I need to tell you. Last night, John phoned Natalie and told her about Derrick. That's why Natalie asked Lee to leave. Johns was concerned about Lee's safety."
Jerome goes silent for a minute. "Well, there's nothing we can do about that now, but just make sure he doesn't tell her about me... okay?"

"You have my word."
From the conversation Jerome heard earlier between Derrick and Lee, he was thankful that she was no longer in the home.

Lee pulled up to the cabin, surprised to see two cars parked where she would normally park.
Who do these cars belong to? She wondered.
Jerome found a spot half a block from the cabin. He positioned himself where he could see the entrance of the cabin. He watched as Lee removed her luggage from her trunk and headed for the front door.
Lee walked up the stairs that lead to the front door. She took her time as she looked around taking in her surroundings. She made it to the front door and inserted the key in the lock.
She opened the door and was halfway in when she spied two male bodies relaxed on the couch in the living room area. Startled when James looked up, she could only stand there in shock.
    "What… this can't be?" she said breathlessly as the two men headed in her direction.
    "I thought you two were dead."
James was the first to embrace her. James hugged Lee and pressed her head against his chest. He was delighted to see her and to know she was okay. James bent down and kissed her lightly on her forehead.
    "Okay, break it up! It's my turn," John said. James grabbed her luggage and headed for one of the guest rooms on the third floor.
    "Come take a seat so I can explain everything to you."
After explaining to Lee, she broke down in tears. She went on to explain about Jason.
John handed her some tissues and hugged her. "We know all about Jason's accident. We know Derrick set him up and believe me… he will pay."
    "I'm afraid for Natalie. Derrick is trying to move in on her."
    "Don't worry about Nat; she can take care of herself. She knows about us. I phoned her last night. That's why she asked you to leave for your safety. Believe me; she did not want you to leave."
Lee was relieved to know James and John were alive and had communicated with Natalie about Derrick.

Chapter Nine

Uninvited Guest

Jerome was just about to pull off and head back to Indy when a black town- car caught his attention. The car slowly crept up the hill and parked across from his cabin. Jerome sat back and waited to see if anyone was going to get out and when they did he recognized a few of Rico's men.

"What the hell!" he yelled as he got on the phone with James. Jerome's fingers tightened in a death grip around the steering wheel. He was furious that they had the nerve to follow Lee up to the cabin. What had they planned on doing to her?

The three men dressed in black got out of the car and head toward the cabin, pistols in hand.

"Hey man, you have three of Rico's men heading your way with guns drawn."

"How far are they?" James asked coolly.

"They're walking across the street as we speak."

"Okay… thanks for the heads up."

James rushed to Lee and took her to the lower level of the cabin.

"Stay here and whatever you do, don't come out. We have uninvited guests that we need to deal with."

Lee was confused. "Uninvited guests?"

Lee had no idea what was going on, as she made herself comfortable on the couch. She grabbed the remote, flicking through the channels until she found a movie to watch. She relaxed watching, 'Set It Off', one of her favorite movies. She kicked her shoe off and propped up the pillow and stretched out on the couch.

The men made their way up the steps that lead to the front of the cabin as Jerome made his way around the side of the cabin that would lead him to the men, thankful for the seclusion and the moonlight that shined, allowing him to see the intruders.

Jerome pulled out his silencer and moved further around the cabin, and with his Bluetooth, he made conversation with James.

"I'm right behind them. I'll take the one in the back, you and John can take the two in front. On the count of three, let's do what we do best." He breathed softly, waiting for the perfect moment. One, two… three."

The only sounds heard were those of bodies hitting the pavement. Jerome shot the intruder in the back of the head. When his friends turned to the sound of him hitting the pavement; James and John shot the other two in the back of their heads. These men had no chance; they had no idea that Jerome was sitting in his car as they pulled up. James and John emerged from the darkness and stood over the dead men.

"Three down, five more to go," Jerome nodded.

"Have you spoken to Ricky about getting him out?" John asked.

"No, I haven't. I'm glad you mentioned it. I'll call him right now."

Jerome dialed Ricky's number. He let it ring four times and hung up. Ricky knew it was Jerome calling. He walked away from the other men and phoned Jerome.

"Hey, what's up?"

"We need to meet to discuss some things. Meet me at the warehouse tomorrow evening around six and make sure no one follows you." Jerome hung up. He didn't want to keep Ricky on the phone for fear of Rico's men becoming suspicious. When Rico's goons don't show up, Jerome knew all hell would break loose.

"Hey, I'm not sure it'll be safe for you guys to continue to hide out here if Rico's men knew Lee was here, I know Rico knows this location, and he'll probably head this way when these bastards don't show up."

"We'll be fine here… and for any more uninvited guests, I wouldn't want to be in their shoes. John and I will do whatever it takes to keep Lee safe," James assured Jerome.

"Now that we have that out of the way, what are we going to do with these bodies," John asked.

Jerome pointed to the back. James and John turned and walked to the back of the cabin that revealed trees that were tall and plentiful hiding the river that flowed downstream.

"The perfect place to dump three bodies. It will be weeks before the bodies are discovered," Jerome declared.

Jerome ran to his car and opened the trunk, digging around for materials he always kept for times like this. He removed some tarps and rope and headed back to where James and John were waiting. "Here wrapped each body in the tarp and tied them up."
Once they were finished, each man took their turn in tossing the bodies in the river. The three men stood above the river and watched as the bodies were carried away downstream.

"How is Lee doing?" Jerome asked.

"Now that she knows the truth about Nat asking her to leave, she's doing okay, but she still mourns the loss of Jason."
Jerome replied. "Well, that's understandable. They've been a part of each other's lives for a long time."

"Just keep her safe, that's all I ask."

"I told you we got this," James smiled a little.

"Well, it looks like my job here is done," Jerome said as he embraced the two men.
James and John walked to the front of the cabin as Jerome walked down to his car. Jerome will head back to Indy for his meeting with Ricky tomorrow.

"Alright boys, make sure you take good care of Lee and keep an eye open for anything unusual. If something doesn't feel right, it's probably not."

"Drive safe." John nodded.

"And don't try and drive straight through, knucklehead." James grinned.

"I won't, I'll drive halfway, then check into a hotel."
Just as he said, Jerome drove for three hours and checked into a hotel for a good night's sleep.
After checking in at the front desk, he headed for the elevator when he ran into someone from his past.

"This can't be happening to me," he said under his breath.

"Hello, Jerome. How have you been?"

"Hello, Porsha. Life has been good to me and you?"

"I've been doing well. I'm no longer married," she said as she flashed her ring- finger at Jerome.
The two stood eyeing each other from head to toe.

"Well." Porsha smiled a little. "Looks like life has been treating you very well," Porsha said.

"Well, you know, I can't complain."

Jerome remembered the last time the two were together. It was the worst time of his life. Porsha broke his heart and he vowed never to get involved with her again, but the way she looked tonight, that might be hard.

Jerome tried to funnel his thoughts to the present and what was at stake.

"It was nice seeing you, Porsha, but it's time for me to turn in," Jerome said as he walked to the set of elevators. He pushed the up button and waited patiently for the elevator doors to open.

"It was nice seeing you as well," Porsha said as Jerome walked away.

Porsha stood and laughed to herself. She knew Jerome had no idea John had contacted her to help the three of them out with a case.

"Um, Jerome looks very good. This is going to be interesting." Porsha strolled to the bar in the hotel. She took a quick glance around the area for a place to sit. She preferred to sit where she can see who came in and out, hoping Jerome will walk through the doors. As she made her way through the crowded room, she spotted a seat at the bar. As she sat down, she noticed it was pretty crowded for a Thursday night.

"What can I get you to drink?" the bartender asked.

"I'll have rum and coke."

"Rum and coke coming up.

Chapter Ten

Thinking under Pressure

Jerome entered his hotel room. It was small, but it would serve its purpose. Jerome placed his keys on the table, removed his clothes and headed for the shower. Again, he found himself thinking about Porsha and how good she looked tonight.

Down in the bar, Porsha sat and waited in hopes of seeing Jerome. Twenty minutes passed and no Jerome. Porsha glanced around the bar trying to take her mind off of Jerome. She looked over at a couple who seemed to be blind to the people in the bar because they were kissing and touching each other like they were inside their hotel room when someone yelled. "Take that shit to your room!" Porsha cracked a smile. "She guessed he was thinking what she was thinking."

Porsha finished her drink and walked out of the bar to the front desk. "I need to get one of your guest room number."

"Miss, it's against company policy for me to give this information out."

"He's expecting me; I simply forgot what room he is in. You witnessed me holding a conversation with him about a half hour ago."

"I know, but I can't give you his room number."

Just so happened, the manager walked up and heard the tail end of the conversation.

"Is there a problem here?"

"Yes, I am trying to get the room number of a friend who is expecting me, but I am being told this is against company policy to give this information out. Your employee witnessed me speaking with your guest so I am a little puzzled as to why she refuses to give me this information. After all, I am a paying guest too."

"What's the guest's name?"

"Porsha gave the manager Jerome's full name and in return, he wrote Jerome's room number on a card and handed it to her.

"Thank you so much," Porsha said as she glanced over at the attendant and gave him a smile.

Porsha took the elevator to the eighth floor. As she got off, she was a little nervous.

"What if he refuses to let me in?" She thought to herself.

Porsha slowly made her way down the hall until she came to room number 825.

Jerome wrapped in his towel headed for the door after he heard a knock. He peeped out the keyhole. "Oh my God."

He opened the door and Porsha walked in and stood in front of him.

"What are you doing here?"

"I was lonely downstairs in the bar, so I decided to come up and keep you company if that's not a problem." Jerome knew this was more than a problem.

"No, make yourself comfortable," he said while his gut told him otherwise. Jerome watched as Porsha walked pass him. He noticed how firm her ass looked in her dress.

"Man, don't go there." His mind told him.

Jerome stood with his back toward the door. Porsha took in every inch of his divine body. From the shape of his Carmel colored biceps, his rock hard ABS, to his defined legs.

Jerome noticed how Porsha was checking him out.

"What is on your mind, Porsha?"

"What makes you think something is on my mind?"

"Because I know you, and I know you didn't come up here just to sit in this little- ass room with me."

Standing to her feet, she kicked her shoes off. She moved closer to Jerome causing him to move backward. He was now with his back pressed against the door, the perfect position for Porsha.

"I was hoping you would come down and join me for a drink. It's been a long time since we've seen each other."

"And as I remember, that's how you wanted it."

"Jerome that was then, now everything has changed."

"You can say that again," Jerome mumbled under his breath.

Jerome ran his hands through his short, wavy hair, afraid to look Porsha in her eyes for fear of her seeing that his attraction to her was still there.

"What we shared six years ago was a mistake. Porsha looked at him. "A mistake, how can you say that Jerome. You loved me and I loved you. The only difference now is that I'm divorced."

"Jerome, look me in my eyes and tell me that you don't have any feelings for me, tell me," Porsha insisted as she planted herself directly in front of Jerome. He grabbed a hold of her shoulders. "Look, no matter what I feel or don't feel for you, nothing can ever become of us. As bad as I want to take you to bed right now, it can't happen."

Porsha smiled, this is just what she wanted to hear. Jerome still had feelings for her. Porsha yanked the bath towel from Jerome's body. She kneeled down before him and in an instant, she had his penis in her mouth.

Jerome tried to free himself from her, but the feeling had taken control.

"Porsha, I'm warning you, you have to stop this nonsense. You don't want this right now." Porsha stopped for a minute only to tell him, "Don't tell me what I want. Porsha removed Jerome's penis from her mouth and stood to face Jerome running the tip of her tongue around his lips.

Jerome was trying hard to fight the urge to kiss her. He lost the fight when she forced his lips apart. Jerome opened his mouth and allowed her tongue to enter. Jerome kissed her with much intensity. He picked her up in one swift movement and laid her on the bed. Jerome began to undress her; he removed her panties with his mouth. He planted kisses to her feet and began to suck on each toe. He moved up to her legs where he kissed his way up until he came to the insides of her thighs. Once he felt her juices seep out, he let his tongue do the talking.

Porsha, unable to stand anymore, pulled for him--- she wanted him, --- inside her.

"Please, Jerome, I can't take it anymore, I want you inside me."

"Alright baby, open up for daddy," Jerome anxiously said as he slid his pole inside her wet, juicy pussy. Jerome gave her one good stroke. The feeling that ran through his body was unbelievable.The way her pussy clamped down on his penis drove him wild. Jerome pulled out quickly and glided slowly up her body until he reached her breast. He let his tongue caress her nipples before inserting it into his mouth. He used both of his palms to secure her breast as he continued to suck. Then without any hesitation, he moved down south of her body, leaving her in agony. He spread the lips of her pussy apart until her clit was visible. He allowed his tongue to bathe her as he went up and down. With his index and middle finger, he inserted them inside of her slowly moving in and out.

"Jerome, please!" Porsha yelled.

Jerome ignored her cries and continued until her body began to shiver uncontrollably. Jerome inserted himself back inside of her hot wet juicy pussy and took her for the ride of her life.

"Come with me baby," Jerome said as the feeling took control of him.

"I'm coming," Porsha said as the thunderous waves of ecstasy set in.

Five minutes later, Jerome lay on his back, unable to speak. Thoughts of his wife filled his head. Jerome removed himself from the bed and headed for the bathroom where he locked the door behind him. He stared at himself in the mirror, "How could I have been so weak," he reprimanded himself.

Standing under the shower, he let the hot water rinse away the smell of sex from his body as he thought about what this could lead to. Trouble nothing but trouble, he thought.

Chapter Eleven

Too Little Too Late

Back at the cabin, James went down to check on Lee. He found her sound asleep. He stopped in his tracks as he sees her breast busting out of her blouse, the shape of her hips and her voluptuous behind.

"Oh my God," he thought to himself as he stood there in awe. He knew there was something about her that captured his heart, but he never thought he would look at her like this. James walked over to the closet and pulled out a blanket. He walked over to where she laid and covered her up without waking her. James stood above her, looking down at the most beautiful woman he had seen in a long time. Too bad she was his best friend's mother.

James looked around for the remote, but he was unable to find it. He walked over to the television, but before he had a chance to turn it off; his phone rang. The caller on the other end of the phone told him about the news bulletin in Indianapolis about an undercover agent that was murdered.
His body was discovered in the White River with two gunshot wounds to the head. Several witnesses passing by heard sounds of gunshots and called the authorities. The agent was later identified as Ricky Carter. 																													James
rushed upstairs to find John, "Man they killed Ricky!"

"What? What are you talking about?" John asked.

"They found his body in the White River. Oh my God, this can't be happening," James ran his hand over his face.
John was stunned. He didn't know what to do at that moment.
John walked over to the window as he ran his fingers through his hair.

"Shit, Jerome said he needed to get him out. Damn this is fucked up, too little too late."

As Jerome stepped out of the bathroom, Porsha was nowhere in sight. Jerome walked over and took a seat on the side of the bed when his phone rang. He looked at the number that showed the call was coming from John.

"What's up?"

"Man, they found Ricky's body in the White River!"

"What? What the fuck are you talking about?"

"It's on all of the local channels in Indianapolis."

"Aw, man, I'm heading back to the cabin. I should be there in two and half hours," Jerome said as he hit the end button.

Jerome was dumbfounded. He couldn't believe Ricky was dead. Now, he had a guilty conscience, he knew he should have pulled him out sooner. Jerome checked out of the hotel, hopped on the interstate and headed for the cabin.

"Shit!" he yelled as he beat his hand against the steering wheel. "I'm sorry Ricky for not getting you out sooner!"

Derrick learned that Ricky had been murdered. He knew he was next if he didn't come up with Rico's money. He walked into Natalie's room and stood at the door, watching as she brushed her hair before she went to bed.

"Natalie, I need the combination to the safe."

"Derrick, I'm not giving you the combination to the safe. Whatever is in that safe belongs to me," she replied as she walked into the bathroom with Derrick on her tail.

"I'm asking you nicely, Natalie… don't make me do something I will later regret."

Natalie turned to look at him. "Derrick, I don't know what your problem is, but I can assure that the money you are referring to is not in the safe."

"Well, give me the combination so that I can be sure."

"No. You will have to take my word."

Derrick raised his hand and struck her across her face.

"What the fuck is your problem!" Natalie cried as she held a hand to her face. The sting from Derrick's hit stunned her. A man had never hit Natalie in her life and today will be the first and last time that a man would, she told herself.

Natalie grabbed a hold of the lamp that was on her nightstand and struck Derrick in the head, causing him to fall to the ground.

Natalie grabbed her purse and keys and ran for the door, but the hit that she gave was not enough to knock him out. As she ran by him, he grabbed her by her once broken ankle, causing her to fall.

"Bitch, what is your problem hitting me in my head? I asked you nicely for the combination, but I see you want to play hard. Well, I can give it to you hard," Derrick grumbled as he threw another punch to her face, knocking her out cold.

When Natalie came to, she was in her bed. She gazed around the room as she heard male voices coming from downstairs. The men were angry. As she continued to listen, they were yelling at Derrick.

"Where's my money, mother-fucker."

"Rico, I need more time," Derrick was pleading.

As Natalie sat in fear, she heard the voices move closer.

"Oh my God, what am I going to do?"

Natalie ran and hid in the hidden closet. She tried to control her breathing before they heard her.

"I promise, I will have your money in two days," Derrick lied to buy himself more time.

"Two days, and don't make me come looking for you either," Rico growled as he pointed his finger at Derrick.

The men walked back downstairs. Natalie waited until she heard the door shut before removing herself from the closet.

She ran and grabbed her cell phone and headed back to the closet and dialed John's number. Just as John answered, Derrick, walked back in the room.

"Natalie! Natalie, are you okay?"

For fear of Derrick hearing John on the other end, she disconnected the call and turned her phone on silent mode.

"Natalie, where are you? I promise I won't hurt you, but now you see how important it is for me to have the combination to the safe. I can assure you that the money is there." Derrick said as he looked around the room for her.

John dialed Natalie's phone back. When she sees it was John, she held the phone to where John could hear Derrick's conversation.

"Natalie, bitch you better come; out. You're making me mad. I don't want to hurt you again, but I will if I have too." Derrick was freaking out. He knew he better come up with Rico's money, or it was the end for him and whatever he and Natalie could ever have.

James and John stood there listening to Derrick. They felt awful that they were not there to protect her.

John cannot take it anymore and dialed Derrick cell.

"You fucking bastard! Touch her again and I will blow your fucking brains out!"

"Who is this? Is this John?"

Derrick looked around the room as if he was waiting for John to appear.

"Who the fuck did you call Natalie? Answer me, you fucking bitch, just wait until I get my hands on you!" Derrick yelled as he continued to search for Natalie.

Derrick threw the cell phone across the room and walked out; he walked down the hall toward the safe that was built in the wall. He fumbled with the combination; he wondered what Jason would have used for the combination. He tried Jason's birthday, then he tried Natalie's birthday… still, it did not open. As he continued to try to open the safe, he noticed a key slot.

"Jackpot, "Derrick yelled. "I'll have a locksmith come over and make a key to the safe. Did you hear that, Natalie?" Derrick said as he rubbed his hands together thinking he was about to find the money.

"Dumb ass," Natalie said to herself.

What Derrick didn't know was that the key slot had been a ploy to throw someone off. The safe did not open with a key or combination. It would only open with Jason or Natalie's thumb print.

Chapter Twelve

An awkward silence

James and John sat and listened to Derrick in the background, the two men were furious that they were not there to rescue Natalie. John decided he could longer sit by while Natalie was in trouble, so he made a dangerous choice to go to Indianapolis to get Natalie before something happened to her.

"I hope you know what you are doing," James said as he stood to face John.

"This could put all of our lives in danger."

"I know, I'll be careful, but I can't sit around and wait to see if what happened to Ricky will happen to Nat--- I just can't do that." As John was about to head out, his phone rang. "Hey Porsha, where are you?"

"I'm right outside the cabin."

"Okay, come on in."

"Porsha is out front and Jerome should be on his way as well. I think you should wait until he arrives."

John ran down to meet Porsha and walked her up to the top level of the cabin where he and James had set up shop.

"Hello Porsha, glad you could make it."

Porsha looked stunned; James had never liked her and always made sure she knew it.

"Hello James, it's good to see you."

Porsha dropped her duffle bag and walked over to James.

"So, what's the plan?"

"We'll discuss that just as soon as Jerome arrives."

Porsha looked around the cabin. Pretty nice she thought. Each floor of the cabin had a fireplace, a flat-screen television and a balcony that was accessible from all of the bedrooms on each floor. The cabin was spacious and very peaceful. She can see why they picked this place to hide out.

An hour later, Jerome phoned James.

"Is the coast clear?"

"Yes, come on up, we've been waiting for you."

When Jerome pulled up, he noticed another vehicle parked out front. He had a good view of James and John, but there was another person in the room with them that he didn't recognize.

Jerome got out of the car with his gun cocked and slowly made his way up the walkway when James walked out.

"Is everything okay inside?"

"Sure, why do you ask?"

"As I pulled up I noticed an unfamiliar car."

"Oh," James said as he laughed. Everything is fine, come on in. There's something I want you to listen to." As Jerome and James head upstairs, Jerome heard a familiar voice.

"It can't be."

As Jerome reached the top step, he stopped when he sees Porsha. He glanced back at James. James shrugged his shoulders, "It wasn't my idea."

Jerome walked into the room, he and Porsha exchanged looks, but no spoken words were passed between the two. An awkward silence came over the room.

"Have a seat," John said as he played the recording back for Jerome to hear.

"Oh hell no, we have got to get her out of that house tonight. John, can you send a message to Natalie letting her know that we are on our way to get her."

"Yes, just as long as Derrick has not gotten to her."

The three stood and waited for Natalie's response. Five minutes go by without a response.

"That's it, let's go. James, I want you and Lee to take her car and go to this address while John and I go to the house to get Natalie. Once we rescue Nat, John will bring her to you and Lee."

"What will I do?" Porsha asked.

"Just sit tight until you hear from me," Jerome said as he walked down the stairs. James and John picked up on the tension between Jerome and Porsha. It was tension in the air that could only be from one thing. John looked at Jerome with an uncanny look. He only hoped it was not what he was thinking, as he shook his head.

Jerome and John hopped in their cars and waited for James and Lee to leave the cabin. Lee was full of questions, "Where are we going and why are we leaving in such a hurry?"

"Just get in the car and I will explain everything to you as I drive." James and Lee head out, "Lee I'm taking you somewhere where you'll be safe. Natalie will join us shortly."

"What do you mean somewhere where I will be safe? I thought I would be safe at the cabin."

"While you were downstairs we had some uninvited guest that followed you up here."

"Oh my, why, does this have anything to do with Jason?"

"Probably so, but don't worry, we have everything taken care of."

"Well, if you took care of the problem, why are we headed somewhere else?"

"It's just a precaution, if they knew you were here then other people may know."
Lee gets quiet as her gut feeling told her that trouble was brewing.

"I hope John knows what he's doing by coming out of hiding. I could have gone and got Nat."

"Lee, the way Derrick feels about you, no way could we allow you to jeopardize your life. We're better suited for things like this or have you forgotten? John and I have years of experience in this field. How many years of experience do you have?" James said as he threw his head back and laughed.
Lee looked over at James, "You are really funny. I'm just glad you and John are here. I only wish my Jason was around," she sighed as she turned to glance out of the window.
James grabbed a hold of her face with one hand and turned her face to look at him. "Jason is with you in spirit. Right now, he's probably right behind us making sure you get where you're going safely." His voice was soft and filled with care. James was feeling a certain kind of way about Lee and he didn't know where it was coming from. At this moment, if he wasn't behind the wheel, he would have probably kissed her. This is how much he was attracted to her. The way he was feeling was really bothering him. He wondered if she was feeling the same way.
Lee smiled as she laid her head back against the headrest. Something about James was making her feel giddy inside. She didn't know what was going on, but one thing was for sure, she was certainly enjoying

it. She snuck a peek at James out of the corner of her eye. Lee was enjoying the way his thighs filled out his jeans and the way his chest and arms looked so defined. Let's not forget about the eyes and his dark brown complexion. His gray eyes set his whole look off.
Lee tried so hard to guide her thoughts elsewhere, but for some reason, they continued to come back to James.

"James, can I ask you a personal question?"

"Sure, go ahead, but I'm not saying I am going to answer it."

"Whatever. Are you in a relationship with anyone, and if so, is it serious?"

James laughed. "Why in the world would you ask me this?" James was hoping she was feeling the way he was.

"Because I want to know, that's why."

"Are you seeing anyone and if so, is it serious?"

Lee turned to look at James and when she did, she sees something that made her heart skip a beat.

"No Lee, I am not seeing anyone. What about you?"

"No, I am single as well."

Out of nowhere, James reached over and grabbed a hold of Lee's hand. The electrifying feeling that ran through both of their bodies when they touched was out of this world. It was so powerful that they both jump when their hands touched.

Lee laid her head back and closed her eyes as images of James danced around in her head.

James smiled as he thought about how Jason would feel if he knew how he felt about his mom.

Jerome and John followed behind Lee and James to make sure they arrived at their exit safely.

Chapter Thirteen

Killing two birds with one stone

Hours later, Lee awoke to the sound of James' voice.

"We're here."

Lee looked up at him and smiled. "Where are we?"

"We are about forty-five minutes outside of Indianapolis. You and Natalie will be safe here."

As Lee entered the condo, the inside smelled of Jason.

"Did this condo belong to Ja---" was all she could say when she sees a picture of Jason and Natalie.

Lee walked over and picked up the picture. She ran her hand across Jason's face as a tear- drop onto the picture. James walked over to where Lee stood and removed the picture from her hand. He set the picture down on the fireplace mantel before hugging her. Lee rested her head against his chest. She felt so at ease when she was around James now. "I could stay let this forever." She whispered.

James thought he heard her say what she said, that she could stay like this forever, but he was not sure.

Assuming by the décor and pictures, James knew this must be Jason's hideaway.

"I know just as much about this place as you do," James said.

"I know this must be so hard for you right now, but believe me, it will get better, I promise, but in the meantime, we should try and make ourselves comfortable until Natalie arrives." James removed himself gently from Lee.

"Yeah, I guess you are right."

Jason Jackson had been working undercover as a drug dealer off and on for the past ten years and was close to taking down one of the biggest drug lords that had set up shop in Indianapolis.

Jason had devoted much of his time to this case for the last year or so until a fellow undercover agent double -crossed him leading up to his death.

Derrick Snow was a dirty, grimy undercover agent who was consumed with greed. Derrick would rat on his own mother if the price were right. Derrick informed Rico that Jason was about to take him and his crew down so Rico had his men take Jason out. Rico and his men learned that Ricky was a part of Jason's team and they eliminated him from the picture as well. This was why John called in Porsha so that she could get close to Rico and be their eyes and ears on the inside.

John and Jerome exit the interstate. Jerome pulled into a gas station and motioned for James to pull up beside him. John did and rolled down his window.

"Hey man, we need to make sure this goes as plan. I can't and won't allow Natalie to be harmed at any cost."

"I'm on the same page," John agreed.
Jerome got out of his car and heads for his trunk. He pulled out two bullet- proof vests and two ski masks.
He threw one to John as he pulled off his shirt and slid the vest over his chest.

"Make sure your mask is on before we turn on the street, just in case we have company. Text Nat and tell her to be prepared to get out. Tell her that we should be there in fifteen minutes. Let her know that when she hears the sound of the blow horn to get out of the house as quickly as she can."

Jerome waited as John sent the text to Natalie. They waited patiently for a response from her. Ten minutes went by and still no response from her. Jerome started to think the worst.

"Let's go!" Jerome growled.
The men hopped into their vehicles and head for Natalie's house. As they pulled onto the street, John pulled over. He had just received a response from Natalie. Jerome pulled along side of John and rolled his window down,

"Natalie finally responded back. She will be waiting for the signal."
Jerome took off his mask and wipe the sweat from his forehead,

"I am getting too old for this bullshit."
John laughed as the two approached the house. Jerome stayed behind just in case there was trouble. John pulled up in front of the house he left the engine running. Jerome parked right behind him and when

John gave him the okay signal, he blew his horn, the sound of the blow horn echoed throughout the neighborhood. John and Jerome sat eagerly waiting for Natalie to exit the house, but what they didn't notice was a white van parked across the street.

Rico and his men had parked outside waiting for the right time to enter the house to murder Derrick and any witnesses. Rico's men were just about to exit the van when Rico motioned them to stay put. Rico noticed two cars pulling up and decided to wait.

Natalie heard the sound of the blow horn and eased her way out of the closet. She had no idea where Derrick was as she crept across the carpet down the hall that led to the stairs. She climbed down each stair carefully until she was on the last step. She could see headlights out of the window, which caused her heart to beat faster. It was like seeing the light down the hall, but the more you walk the further it got from you.

Natalie finally made it to the front door, she took a deep breath as she slid the door slightly open. She looked back to see if Derrick was in sight, then she moved further out of the door, but just as she had her body out the door, the door was yanked open.

"Where the fuck do you think you are going?"

Natalie tried to run, but Derrick was right on her tail, he grabbed a hold of her hair and threw her to the ground. Just then, John and Jerome hopped out of their cars, guns in hand and ran to Natalie's rescue. Jerome threw a kick that caught Derrick under his chin; making him fall backward. He reached for his gun that had fallen when he grabbed Natalie. Jerome yelled to John trying to disguise his voice, "Get her out of here!"

"Who the hell are you?" Derrick was trying to struggle to his feet.

"I am her knight in shining armor, mother-fucker," Jerome said, as he fired a bullet that hit Derrick straight in the chest.

Derrick never had a chance. He was going to be taken down by Jerome or Rico's men, but either way, he was going to die.

As Derrick fell to the ground, Jerome ran and hopped in his car to catch up to John and Natalie.

Chapter Fourteen

Payback's a bitch

Rico and his men sat in the van and watched as if they were watching an action movie.

"Well, it looks like someone has taken care of our dirty work for us," one of Rico's men said.

"I know, but who are they? Follow that car; I want to see where they're going and who they are," Rico demanded.

"Something doesn't seem right with those two men. If I didn't know any better, I would think it was Jason and one of his buddies." In the meantime, John phoned James to let him know that he and Natalie were on their way and should be there shortly.

Rico and his men continued to follow Jerome for about an hour.

"How long are we going to follow this dude and what does he have to do with us?"

Rico finally told his man to exit the interstate and head back to Natalie's to retrieve Derrick's body. The driver shook his head,

"You mean to tell me I have been following this dude for an hour and now you want to me to go back to the house?"

"Yeah, do you have a fucking problem with that?" Rico shouted.

"No, boss, not at all," the driver said sarcastically. "Stupid son of a bitch," the driver said under his breath. The driver, known as Tommy boy, grew tired of Rico's tactics. He had been plotting a way out, but every time he got a chance to leave town, Rico's came up with a job for him to do. If only someone would put a bullet through his big thick head, all of his problems will be over.

As Tommy turned the corner on Natalie's street, they noticed several of the neighbors were standing out on the sidewalk talking. Tommy made his way down the street and stopped two houses down. Rico instructed. "Turn the ignition off. We'll sit here and wait until these noisy mother-fuckers go back inside."

They continued to sit when they see the neighbors walking down the street to their houses. They waited until they went inside before exiting the van. When they approached the house, the first thing that

they noticed was that Derrick's car was missing. The men walked up to the front door and knocked a couple of times before Tommy turned the knob and the door opened. The men enter the home and check the downstairs the second and third floor, but there was no sight of Derrick. "Where could this mother-fucker be?
Rico shouted rubbing his head, "What the hell is going on?"

"Maybe Derrick was able to drive himself to the hospital," Tommy boy said.

"When we get back to the house, I want you to call all the nearby hospitals to see if he showed up at any of them."
Tommy exhaled loudly.

"Is there something you want to get off your chest?" Rico asked Tommy?
Tommy boy ignored Rico and headed back to the van.

"That's what I thought," Rico uttered.

Porsha awoke and glanced around at her surroundings. She got up from the couch and walked over to the window. The sun was slowly rising and still no word from the guys. Porsha decided to call Jerome she dialed his number and waited for him to answer, but the call went to voicemail, she began to panic. She was stuck in the cabin with no idea where the guys were so it was not as if she could go and search for them. All she knew is that they were going to rescue someone by the name of Natalie.
All of a sudden a light goes off in her head, "What about the condo?"
Porsha dialed the number and on the fourth ring, James answered.

"James, thank God you're okay!"

"Porsha, is that you?"

"Yes, James it's me. Thanks for keeping me updated on what's going on."

"I'm sorry Porsha, everything has been taken care of, we'll be here in Indy for a day or two, but Jerome is on his way back to the cabin."

"Good, just what I wanted to hear. I guess I will see you and John when you get here." She said as she rushed off the phone.
Porsha heads for one of the rooms in the back. She went through her duffel and removed a black thong and one of her short night-- shirts. She goes into a separate compartment and pulled out her deodorant, and the usual necessities before heading down the hall to the

bathroom. Porsha massaged her body down with the shower gel as she sang a song from Keisha Cole's latest CD, 'Woman to Woman'.

"Heard you say that you just need a real woman. Baby, here I come. I hear you, baby. Had some mishaps and a couple setbacks, baby here I am, I hear you, baby, open up your door, I really need to come, I need it all, won't be no frontin I hear you call I'm bringing the loving yeah, gotta have you in my life. I will be losing my mind every time you take me to your wonderland. When I look into your eyes I get lost in your wonderland."

After rubbing her body down with lotion, Porsha slipped on her thong and her night--shirt and lay across the bed waiting for Jerome's return.

Porsha awoke to the sound of running water. She hopped out of bed and grabbed the gun that lay underneath the pillow. Porsha listened for any movement in the cabin before peering out the window. As she glanced out, she sees Jerome's car parked out front.

"Thank God," she said quietly as she walked over to the dresser and placed the gun down. She made her way back to the bed and removed her night shirt and thong as she lay there in silence, debating on how to get Jerome to make love to her.

Several minutes later, Jerome walked down the hall to the room adjacent to her room without glancing in her direction. Porsha moved off the bed and stood in the doorway appalled that Jerome walked right by her room without saying a word. Not able to take the stillness she made her way in front of his door. She turned the knob and slowly pushed his door open.   Porsha stared at the masculine body wrapped in a dark blue towel. She licked her lips, she needed some of that… right now."

Porsha walked further into Jerome's room, with his back toward her. She snuck up behind him and wrapped her arms around his waist. Jerome stood still. He heard the sound of his door opening, but hesitated to turn in the direction of the sound. He positioned himself with his gun ready to take out who was behind him when he felt arms wrapping around him. When he turned, he found Porsha standing there.

"Woman, what is wrong with you sneaking up on me like that?"

"I'm sorry, did I scare you, sweetheart?" Jerome looked at Porsha and shook his head.

"Jerome, I have missed you so much."

Porsha stood on her tippy toes and kissed Jerome under his chin. She moved her way up and kissed him on his lips. Jerome moved his head and grabbed her by the arms, not allowing her to move. He bent his head down and circled her areola with his tongue before taking her nipple into his mouth.

Porsha removed her arms from his hold and removed the towel exposing his body and the profused pole that she craved. Porsha moved down Jerome's body and stopped at his midsection, where she took her tongue and ran it across his head. She slid her tongue up and down the side of his penis before taking him into her mouth. Jerome stood unable to move, the feeling was enough to curl his toes. He rolled his eyes back in his head as the feeling of Porsha's lips wrapped around him while her hand massaged his balls.

"Oh my God," Jerome groaned.

Jerome found the strength to pull away from her and pulled her up; he grabbed her by the butt cheeks and lifted her off the floor. Porsha quickly spread her legs and wrapped them around his waist. Jerome lay Porsha down on the bed and buried his head between her legs, he continued to torture her until she can't take anymore. He entered her with one hard, thrust, moving in and out deeper and deeper until they both exploded with pleasure.

Jerome collapsed on the bed and Porsha moved closer to snuggle right next to him. The two lay there in silence before Porsha looked up at Jerome.

"Jerome, we need to talk about us."

Jerome rose his exhausted body to a sitting position "Us? What do you mean us? There is no us, I'm a married man now. When I wanted it to be us you wanted something different."

"What? Why didn't you tell me this in the beginning? Why did you fuck me just now if you're married?"

"You didn't ask. You just assumed that I was the same pussy-whipped man that I used to be."

"And you just proved to me that you still are the same pussy-whipped man. Obviously, your wife is not doing her job... if so, it wouldn't have been so easy to get you to fuck me."

"Leave my wife out of it. My wife does her job just fine."

"Yeah, I bet."

"Don't go getting your feelings twisted about me. This time I am the poison." Jerome eased off the bed and headed for the bathroom.

"I can't believe this shit!" Porsha yelled at his back and threw a pillow at Jerome as he walked out of the room.

"Payback's a bitch!" Jerome yelled down the hall loud enough for Porsha to hear.

Porsha hopped off the bed and stood in the hallway. "You got that right, payback can be a bitch," Porsha yelled back.

Unfortunately, Jerome was already in the bathroom with the door closed, unable to hear her last remark.

Porsha was Jerome's everything and she knew it, she played on his emotions and used this to get whatever she wanted from him, but this time, things were different. He had the upper hand and a relationship with her was not in the cards. Jerome was happily married, but due to circumstance out of his control, he could not be with the woman he loved right now.

Jerome wanted badly to pay Porsha back for the way she had treated him and now he had gotten his pay back, but as Porsha said, payback can be a bitch.

Chapter Fifteen

Tension among Friends

James and John arrived at the cabin the next day. James can sense the tension between Porsha and Jerome.

"Jerome, can I speak to you for a minute?"
Jerome and James head out on the back deck.

"I know you're a grown man and you might think this is none of my business, but I hope what I'm sensing is not going on between you and Porsha?"
Jerome stiffened "You're right, I'm a grown ass man, and it is none of your business what I do or don't do."
James threw his hands up to surrender, "Okay, I'll stay out of it. I just hope you know what you're getting yourself into."
James headed back inside, leaving Jerome alone on the deck. Jerome knew James was right. He knew he had his best interest at heart and that he had no right to talk to his good friend the way he did. He felt bad betraying his wife when the situation was already difficult for her as it was.
Jerome ran his hand through his hair as he made his way back inside. As he entered, John gave him a look of disgust and James ignored his presence.

"I guess you want to tell me how to live my life as well."

"No, I'm going to stay out of it and hope you do the right thing by your wife. I would hate to see you lose her over someone who is not worth it… but you should already know that."

"You guys don't understand, I needed to do this. When this is all over, I will sit down and talk with the two of you, but right now, I need for you guys to be understanding of me and my actions."

"Oh, so we should just sit around while you cheat on your wife. Haven't you put her through enough as it is?" James responded.

"Man, I am losing my fucking mind not being able to be with her right now, and paying Porsha back is helping me get through this difficult time."

"Don't let your payback bite you in your ass," John remarked.

"It's over. I did what I needed to do. James, you of all people know how bad she did me. It affected me in ways I never thought it would, it even affected my marriage the first two years. I started to believe that I wasn't worthy of having someone love me. It took several years before I realize that my wife loved me with all her heart and no matter what Porsha told me about myself, my wife didn't see me that way."

James and John were stunned. They never knew Porsha was the one that hurt him, but they were well aware that someone years ago had broken his heart… but to them, no matter how bad she hurt him, this was no reason to sleep with her and betray his wife.

"I just wish you would have done something different to get back at her," James said.

"How do you feel about her now?" John asked.

"I have no feelings for her. When I fucked her, I envisioned myself making love to my wife."

After eavesdropping on the men's conversation, Porsha can't stand to hear anymore and made her presence known.

"Are you guys finished talking about me?"

"Pretty much," Jerome said.

Porsha gave Jerome an evil eye as she took a seat across from him.

"So... what's my assignment?"

Jerome fumbled through a folder that lay across the table. He pulled out a picture of Rico and handed it to her.

"I need you to get close to this man here."

"And how should I do this?"

"He hangs out at a well-known club in Indy. He likes spending money on pretty women with big breasts and ass. I want you to get him to trust you, trust you enough to bring you home. Once you get inside, I need you to be our eyes and ears. I need to know when the biggest drug deal will go down. Can you do that?"

"Does that mean I have to fuck him?" She asked, putting an emphasis on the word fuck.

"If that's what it takes."

"I guess he'll appreciate this good shit."

Jerome laughed, "If you say so, I guess he will."

James and John stood listening to the play back and forth between Jerome and Porsha. They wondered if Jerome was truly over Porsha. For his sake, they hoped he was."

"Is there anything, in particular, I should wear for my meeting with Mr. Rico?"

"Wear anything that shows that ass," Jerome said as he rubbed his hand over his manhood.

"I'm going to need some spending money to buy some new clothes and money for a hotel until I convince Rico to move me in with him."

"What do you mean 'move you in with him'?"

"Now Jerome, you know once I put this good shit on him, he's going to want me around all the time." Porsha said as she rubbed herself between the legs.

"I guess I should go put on my long boots because the shit in here is getting too deep for me," James said as he looked at John.

"I agree," John replied as he followed behind James into the next room.

As Porsha prepared to leave, Jerome pulled her to the side.

"Once you get inside his home, I want you to put these four bugs in areas of his home where the most conversations take place. Save one to put in his vehicle. I want to hear everything that goes on."

"So should I put one in the bedroom so that you can hear us when we fuck?"

Jerome grabbed her wrist. "Make sure you don't fuck that nigga, the way you fucked me."

"Do I detect a bit of jealousy?"

Jerome let go of her and started to walk away, "By the way, I need for you to check in with me on a daily basis."

Chapter Sixteen

The truth revealed

Later that night, Jerome stood alone on the deck. He took in the quiet sound and the moonlight that shined in the sky. The cool breeze that brushed up against his face as he stood there thinking. In his mind, this had been just a job… but if he was true to himself, he knew he was still very much in love with Porsha. He wondered how this could be; how can a man be in love with two women at the same damn time. He never thought this was possible, but this was a prime example of a man in love with two women.

So caught up in his thoughts, he didn't hear James and John as they stepped out onto the deck.

"Hey buddy, you've got it bad. What are you going to do about it," James asked as he pats Jerome on the back.

"Man, I don't know what to do. I thought I was over her, but when we were talking about her and Rico, I was actually jealous that she's going to be spending time with another man. I thought getting back at her would relieve any feelings that I had for her, but instead, they've made them stronger than before."

"I knew, in the beginning, bringing her in was a bad idea, but John, on the other hand, disagreed with me."

"Well, at the time I thought it was a good idea, but now I know it's a mistake. Jerome, I apologize for bringing someone in, from your past. I never knew it was her."

"What's done is done. I'll have to get some self-control when it comes to Porsha. I'm a grown man who should be able to walk away from some good pussy."

The men stand around drinking until the cool breeze was too much so they move their conversation inside. James stood at the window looking out as John and Jerome relaxed on the couch.

"What's got you so quiet tonight James?" Jerome asked.

"Oh, just thinking about some things," There is no way he can tell Jerome what he's really thinking about and keep their friendship intact. James moved over to the recliner, plopped down and pulled the lever back, and relaxed as his mind stayed on Lee.

"You know, it seems funny that I know you two like the back of my hand," John said as he looked at James. "And I would swear on my life that your quietness now has something to do with a woman." Jerome threw his head back and laughed. "That's impossible. Not the ladies' man over there. Man, you have more women than any of us running behind you like a dog in heat and you pay no attention to any of them. So who is she?" Jerome asked.

"Since you guys know so much, why don't you tell me?"

"Come on man, we're like brothers here. Don't keep us in the dark," John smiled.

"You two have no idea what you're talking about. There is no woman," James laughed at the two as he made his way to his bedroom.

Inside his room, he pondered about calling Lee. He thought that if he talked to her it will help get her off his mind. James pulled out his cell phone and dialed Lee's number and lets it ring three times before deciding to hang up. He knew it was a bad idea.

Two minutes later, his cell phone rang. "Hello Lee, how are you?"

"I'm fine James, how are you?"

"I've been better. Are you and Natalie okay? You haven't seen anything unusual have you?"

"No, we're fine and everything has been quiet around here. Should we be worried?"

"Oh no, you guys are safe, I promise."

The two sit on the phone in silence. They both danced around the feeling that they both felt for each other.

"Well, I guess I'll let you get some sleep. If you need me, Lee, don't hesitate to call me."

Lee almost told James that she needed him right now, but decided against telling him how she really felt at the moment.

"Okay James, thank you and good night."

"Good night, Lee."

Jerome lay in bed thinking about the mess around him. He thought about his wife and hoped she was safe. He missed her and can't wait until the day they could be reunited, but on the other hand, there was Porsha. What was he going to do about her? He was torn between a woman who was meant for him and a woman who made him feel a way that no woman has ever made him feel. Jerome fell asleep, he tossed and turned all through the night. His soul was restless and it was all because of Porsha's re-entry into his life. Jerome dreamed of Porsha; he dreamed that she was underneath him as he caressed her body from head to toe as she cried out for him to take her to a new level of ecstasy. Jerome awoke immediately to find himself alone. He dragged himself out of bed into the restroom where he relieved himself.

Porsha lay awake in her hotel room, thoughts of Jerome filled her head. Jerome never knew the truth behind Porsha's hurtful words and action toward him. She truly loved him and to this day, she still did…, but because of her husband's threats against Jerome, she was forced to part ways with him without his knowledge.

Porsha knew about Jerome's marriage, she knew the day that he got married, but she had no idea that he was still married until today. It tore her up inside to learn that the man she loved was marrying someone else, but there was little she could do about it. Porsha's husband had her on lockdown ever since he found out about her affair with Jerome. Her only escape was when she found the nerve to take his life and after she was cleared of any wrong--doing then, and only then, was she able to free herself to be with Jerome. She knew it was going to take some doing to get him to leave his wife, but she would wait until he realized he cannot live without her and if it never came to that, she would accept it and move on.

The next morning, Porsha rose early; she was three hours away from Indianapolis. She decided to continue her drive, check into a hotel, and go shopping with the money Jerome had given her. As she made her way out of the hotel her phone rang. She looked at the number and saw it was Jerome calling.

"Good morning Jerome."

"Good morning. Did I wake you?"

"No, I just checked out of the hotel and was headed to Indy."

Jerome was silent; he was trying to get his thoughts together.

"Are you okay, Jerome?"

"Yes, I'm fine. Porsha, I want you to be careful. If Rico finds out that you're there to spy on him, it could get ugly for you. I want you to call me if things get out of hand or if you don't feel safe."

" Oh Jerome, you do care about me."

Jerome chuckled.

"Woman you know I still care about you, but right now, my life is complicated. I love my wife dearly and in no way do I want to hurt her, but I can't deny my feelings for you. I want you so bad right at this minute, I know it's not right to think the things that I am thinking right now, but I can't get you out of my mind. I can't get the way you felt yesterday when I was buried deep inside you."

"Jerome, if you keep talking like that, I will turn my car around and head back to the cabin. Is that what you want?"

"Yes, but you have a job to do, so just be careful, okay. I'll talk to you later."

Porsha sat in her car debating on whether she should return to the cabin to be with Jerome or continue her drive to Indianapolis as planned. Jerome wanted her and this meant more to her than he would ever know.

Chapter Seventeen

Dressed to Impress

Porsha walked through the club turning heads as she made her way to the bar. She chose a tight- fitting red dress that showed just enough cleavage and every inch of her body. She had a man to catch and with this dress, she would do just that. As she glanced around the club, she noticed five, big men sitting at a table in the corner who looked to be bodyguards, but Rico was nowhere in sight. She ordered her a drink and waited for Rico's arrival when a tall, slender man with salt and pepper hair approached.

"What is a beautiful woman like you sitting in a bar alone?" Not wanting to be bothered, she lied, "I'm meeting my husband here if you don't mind."

"What kind of husband would keep his beautiful wife waiting alone in a place like this?"

"A husband that trusts his wife."

As she continued to try and blow this guy off, she sees Rico coming through the doors.

"Not bad," she thought. Now I just have to find a way to get acquainted. Porsha excused herself from the man at the bar and headed for the ladies room. She walked by Rico's table, making sure she got his attention. She dropped her purse, bent down to pick it up, making sure he got a good view of her breasts.

Rico's eyes follow her from the time she bent down until she entered the ladies room. Once she was inside, she went to the last stall and went in to call Jerome. Jerome picked up on the second ring.

"Hey, I just wanted to let you know I'm at the club and Rico just arrived."

"How many of his goons are there with him?"

"I counted five, are there more?"

"No, Man, I wish I had come to Indy with you. This would be the perfect time for me to get into his home. Oh well, I can't do anything about it now. Just remember to place those devices in the places that we discussed. Let me know once that's been accomplished and be careful. Oh, I almost forgot, what hotel are you staying at and what's your room number?"

"I am staying at the JW and my room number is 510... why?"

"I just wanted to know. Keep me posted."

Porsha checked herself out in the mirror and re-applied her lipstick before making her way out of the ladies room to find Rico standing along the wall. As she attempted to walk pass, he moved in front of her. "Don't I know you?"

"No, I don't think so."

"My name is Rico Lorenz."

"It's my pleasure to meet you, Mr. Lorenz. My name is Porsha Stevens."

" The pleasure is all mines. Would you care to join me for a drink?"

Porsha smiled sweetly "I would love to."

Rico escorted her back to his table. When they arrived, his goons were nowhere in sight.

The two sat and talked for hours. Porsha was actually enjoying his company.

"Why don't you join me for a night- cap at my place?"

"I would love to."

Rico escorted her to his black town car where his driver awaited. The driver, a tall, heavy dark-skinned man, hopped out of the car when he sees Rico approaching and opened the back door.

"Charlie, take us home."

The driver nodded his head, hopped back into the car and headed in the direction of Rico's home.

The two rode in silence, Porsha was trying to figure out how she could place the bug under the seat without drawing Rico's attention. Porsha eased over a little closer to Rico, she placed one hand on his chest and reached up to kiss him on the lips. Rico pulled her closer to him and lunged his tongue into her mouth.

Porsha removed the bug out of her purse with one hand, but it dropped to the floor. Rico removed his tongue from her mouth and looked at her.

"Are you comfortable?"

"No, not really," she said as she moved back to her original position.

This was not going to be easy, she thought to herself. The bug was somewhere on the floor of the car. She could only hope she could get to it before they arrived at Rico's. The last thing she wanted was for one of his men to find it.

Porsha glanced out the window and took in the scenery and had no idea where she was heading, but from the look of the homes that they had passed, she knew Rico lived in an upscale neighborhood.

Finally, they arrive at their destination. The iron gates opened as the black town car pulled into the driveway. The driveway was long and miles from the house. The house itself sat back upon a hill surrounded by trees.

"I hope I know what I'm getting myself into," she said under her breath as she exited the car.

As Porsha got out, she bent down to grab the bug that she dropped on the floor.

"Did you lose something?" Rico asked.

Porsha tried to play it off; she prayed that neither Rico nor his men found the bug before she had a chance to retrieve it.

"I thought part of my earring fell off, but I guess not."

As Porsha entered the house, she was amazed. The house was like something out of a magazine.

Rico led her down a long hall until they came to a set of glass doors, he opened them and ushered her inside. The room looked more like a private club. In the center of the room was a dance floor with a stripper- pole and behind the pole was a fully-stocked bar. To the left was a seating area and to the right are several poker tables. Rico guided Porsha inside to the left to the seating area.

"Would you like a drink?"

"Yes, I would love some wine."

"Wine it is."

As Rico made drinks, Porsha was able to stick a bug in one of the lamps on the end table. She only hoped this room was used frequently.

Rico made his way back to Porsha drinks in hand. Rico took a seat next to Porsha.

"How is it that I have never seen you in the club before?"

"I am not from Indiana. I'm from Cincinnati here on business."

"May I ask what type of business are you here on?"

"I work for a consulting firm out of Ohio. A couple of my business partners and I are here for about two months while we help a newly formed company get up and running."

"And what is the name of that company?"

"It's called Ohio's Best Consulting Firm."

"I've never heard of it. I am very familiar with Ohio and its businesses. How long has Ohio Best Consulting firm been in existence?"

"For about two years now."

Rico sat his drink down on the table in front of them. "Come here." He told Porsha. Porsha moved closer to him. Rico rubbed the back side of his hand down Porsha's face before brushing his lips across hers. He outlined her lips with his tongue before parting her lips. Porsha opened her mouth and allowed Rico to enter. Rico moved his hands to her breast and began to rub her nipple until it became hard. Rico broke the kiss and moved to stand. He reached down for Porsha. "Let's continue this upstairs."

Chapter Eighteen

Mind over matter

Jerome was headed to Indianapolis he felt it was only right for him to be close by just in case trouble arose between Rico and Porsha. Jerome drove straight through and arrived just as the sun was coming up. He checked into the JW and got a room directly across from Porsha's. Thoughts ran through his mind to join her in bed, but decided against it. Little did he know Porsha had not made it back from Rico's.

Porsha turned over to find Rico sitting up in bed, glancing down at her.

"Good morning sweetheart. Did you sleep good?"

"Good morning. Yes, I did," Porsha purred as she smiled up at Rico.

"Are you hungry?"

"Yes, but I have a splitting headache."

"I have a cure for both. I'll have Janet make us some breakfast and have her fix you a bloody Mary for your hangover---I mean your headache." Rico laughed as he got out of bed and headed for the shower.

"You're welcome to join if you want!" he yelled from the bathroom.

Porsha rose up and took in her surroundings. She felt like someone famous waking up in such a large lovely room. The wood burning fireplace was lite that brought some warmth to the room. The extra-long king size bed was so soft and comfortable that she could lay in it for days. The décor was definitely designed by a female. The French doors that lead to the balcony look like they've been dipped in gold. The brown colored walls gave the room a look of elegance.

Porsha eased out of bed and dragged her body into the bathroom with Rico. She let the warm water run down her body as she took in all of Rico's body. He was simply gorgeous she was thinking, from the top of his head to the bottom of his feet. Porsha had never been with anyone so stunning. It was a little intimidating to her.

Porsha moved closer to Rico. She ran her hand through is jet black, silky wavy hair.

"How is it that someone of your stature is single?"

"Who said I was single?" Rico laughed.

"What?"

"Who said I was single? I have a wife. I know you didn't think I was bringing you home with me to be my main lady?"

"Well, I didn't think a man with a wife would bring me to his home."

"Oh, don't get it twisted sister… this isn't my main home. I would never bring another woman where my wife lays her head. She is the Queen -Bee. I would never disrespect her like that."

"We will see," Porsha whispered under her breath.

Porsha goes to work. She did what she was best at and that was turning men out. Once she was finished with Rico, he won't know what hit him. "Oh, and about Queen -Bee, that will soon be me."

It was one in the afternoon when Porsha strolled into the hotel. She was still so on her high- horse from turning Rico out as she walked through the lobby of the hotel that she never saw Jerome sneak up on her from behind.

"Are you just now getting in?"

Porsha Jumped. "Damn, Jerome! Why are you sneaking up on a sister like that?"

"That means you are not on top of your game if I am able to sneak up on you. Don't tell me you fell for this guy? It looks like he has your nose wide open."

"Whatever, I will have you know I turned his ass out so he is the one with his nose wide open."

Jerome laughed to keep from letting Porsha know he was jealous.

"So were you able to plant the devices in the places that we talked about?"

"It's done."

"Good. Would you like to go to lunch?"

"Sure, but let me change into something more comfortable."

Porsha and Jerome head for her hotel room so she could change clothes, but Jerome had something different on his mind.

Porsha slid the card into the slot and waited for the green signal. The two entered the room. Porsha tossed her bags on the couch as she headed for the bedroom.

"You can make yourself comfortable."

Jerome followed Porsha to the bedroom and moved behind her.

"Tell me about your night." He whispered as he grinds on her from behind. Porsha leaned her head back against his chest and guided his hands to her breast. "It was interesting; you didn't tell me Rico was so stunning."

"That ugly mother-fucker."

"Oh, jealousy does not become you, Jerome."

"Jealous my ass, he hasn't got nothing on this big dick nigga right here."

"Boy, boo," Porsha laughed lightly as she walked further into the bedroom.

"So, are you telling me his dick is bigger and better than mine even with my curve?"

"You didn't hear me say anything."

Jerome started to undress.

"Jerome what are you doing. I thought we were going out to lunch?"

"I am lunch, baby."

She couldn't deny that Jerome turned her own. Porsha knew she was going to have to tread lightly with both men because it would be too easy to lose herself to both men.

Jerome lay in bed with his pole in hand as he stroked himself up and down which was turning Porsha on. Porsha undressed quickly and joined Jerome in bed. "Baby let me take care of that."

She started to make circles around the head with her tongue and licked the tip.

"Damn, that feels so damn good. Go ahead and do your thing, Mommie."

Porsha licked the sides of his penis and made her way to his balls. She licked each one slowly. She began to move down and began to lick his asshole. She inserted two fingers inside which caused Jerome to jump.

"Lay back baby and relax. Let me do my thing." Jerome did as she asked and tried to relax. Within minutes, Porsha was fingering his ass while giving him the best head ever.

"Oh Jesus, please, baby don't stop!"

Porsha moved in and out of his ass hole while continuing to slob on his knob. Jerome's eyes rolled back in his head, his toes curled while tears roll down the sides of his face. This was the best feeling he had ever experienced.

This felt so good to Jerome that he thought he was about to shit on himself.

After busting the best nut ever, Jerome lay in silence as Porsha made her way to the bathroom. When she came out, she had a warm wash cloth that she used to wash Jerome down below.

Still stunned from the experience, Jerome still lay in silence.

Then out of nowhere, he spoke, "Damn that was a powerful nut. Woman, what are you trying to do to me?" He rose up and eased off the bed.

"I'm turning that ass out. You thought my sex game was off the chain years ago, I was just holding back from you. Now, I am letting it all go." She smiled and started brushing her teeth in front of the vanity.

"Do you still want to go to lunch?" Porsha asked as she walked over to stand in front of Jerome.

Jerome looked up at her and nodded his head yes.

Chapter Nineteen

Overwhelmed

Rico went home to the wife, but once he was there, he looked at her in a different way. How can a woman he just met make him want to spend the rest of his life with her? The conversation they had was good, but the sex blew him away. His wife had never made him feel the way Porsha had and to be honest, if she wanted to stay being his wife, she had better step her sex game up… if not, Porsha would be the new Queen-Bee.

During lunch, Jerome thought about Porsha's statement about her turning him out. He was going back and forth in his head if he should quit while he could, but the other part of him was curious and wanted to explore more with her.

"What's on your mind, Jerome, You've been so quiet?"

"Oh, I'm just thinking about some things.

How did it go last night?" Jerome asked as he took a sip of his ice-tea.

"It went better than expected." She said as she smiled, remembering how good Rico looked undressed.

"The way we hit it off, I guarantee he will be calling me wanting to get together."

"Just remember what we're trying to accomplish," Jerome remarked in an off-hand way, trying to hide his jealousy.

"Are you worried that I might fall for Rico?"

Jerome sat and stared at Porsha. He was trying to figure out if she was serious or just trying to make him more jealous.

"You're funny, you know," Jerome said as he chuckled.

"No, I think I'm a little more than funny."

Porsha's phones rang. Without looking, she knew who was calling.

"What did I tell you? Hello Rico, how are you?"

"I would be doing a lot better if you were here with me."

"Oh, don't go getting things twisted, you're married, remember?' Porsha said as she laughed.

"Oh, I see," Rico returned.

"When do you want to get together?"

"How about dinner tonight, I can send my driver to pick you up." Porsha rattled off the address of the hotel.

"What time should I expect your driver?"

"How does six o'clock sound?"

"Sounds good, I'll see you then." Porsha ended the call.

"He's like putty in my hands," She grinned as she looked directly into Jerome's eyes and winked.

"What I want you to do without causing Rico to become suspicious is to get him to talk about what it is that he does for a living. Also, pay close attention to the men around him and the things they say. They might talk in codes and if this is the case, try and remember any code words. I'll be close by so if you don't feel safe, send me a 911 text. I want Rico to be so consumed with you that he starts slipping and when he does, I will be right there to take his ass down."

"I hope you're right Jerome."

"Let's go back to the hotel. There's something I want to take care of."

On the ride back, Jerome could not contain himself. He slid his hand between Porsha's thighs, thankful for her dress. He slid her panties to the side and searched for her nub.

Porsha spread her legs wider, giving Jerome more access.

Jerome removed his hand. He licked his middle and index finger and put them back between her legs. He gently massaged her nub up and down he wanted badly to replace his fingers with his tongue.

Jerome reached over to kiss Porsha.

"Watch out Jerome!" Porsha yelled as a pickup truck was headed right for them. Jerome grabbed the steering wheel just in time to weave out of the way of the truck.

"What the hell are you thinking? You could have gotten us killed."

"Damn woman you got me so fucked up in the mind right now."

Jerome didn't like the hold that Porsha had on him. He had got to get control of the situation before it was too late.

They rode back to the hotel in silence. Jerome was pissed with himself.

How can I be so damn stupid that I almost caused us to have an accident?

Once they arrived, Jerome let Porsha out in front of the hotel while he went to park in the parking garage.

"Porsha hit me up before you leave your room."
Porsha looked at Jerome without saying a word and walked in and headed for the elevator. Her mind was clouded with thoughts of how sexy Rico looked this morning.
Porsha entered her room. She checked the clock on the wall.

"Good I have a few hours to relax before Rico's driver arrives."
Porsha head for the bathroom. She ran her bath water, added a little Victoria's Secret Forbidden Vanilla bubble bath to the water. The aroma filled the entire room. Porsha removed her clothing and eased into the water. The water was so relaxing that she laid her head back and before she knew it, she is asleep.
An hour later she awoke to her cell phone ringing. "Oh my God, how long have I been in here?" She asked herself out loud.
Porsha hopped out of the tub, grabbed her bathrobe and rushed to her phone, but by the time she got to it, the caller had hung up. She didn't recognize the number so she didn't call the number back. If it was important, she guessed he or she would call back. Porsha walked back in the bathroom and dried herself off and let the water out of the tub. She still felt a little tired, so she hurried to lotion her body and picked out an outfit to wear before getting into bed to take another short nap.

Jerome sat in his hotel room lonely. He missed his wife right now and would do anything to be with her. He felt guilty about sleeping with Porsha and vowed that he will never step outside his marriage again. Jerome lay across his bed and waited patiently for Porsha's call.

Chapter Twenty

Too much to handle

Porsha phoned Jerome twenty minutes before heading down to the lobby to wait for Rico's driver. She was anxious to be with Rico. Rico had money and power, which turned her on and it didn't help that he was a piece of eye candy and knew how to work with what was between his legs....

By the time Porsha reached the lobby, she sees Rico's driver pulling up to the hotel's entrance and noticed Jerome was parked about two feet away from the entrance. Porsha quickly made her way to the exit and met the driver before he had a chance to come inside. The driver hopped out and opened the passenger door for Porsha. Porsha's heart began to beat rapidly when she sees Rico.

"Good evening," Rico said in his sexiest voice.

"Good evening to you too," Porsha responded as she reached over to kiss him on the lips.

"Oh, your lips are so soft. You know what you did to me last night and this morning? Babe, if you keep that up, you're going to give Mrs. Lorenz a run for her money."

"Honey, I aim to please." she silkily replied as she rubbed him between his legs.

"Now you know I want more than that."

Rico pulled Porsha on top of his lap. Her ass was now sitting directly on his penis. Rico spread her legs apart as he slid his hands up her thighs until he reached her pussy. Luckily for him, she was panty-less.

"Oh! Just like I like it... easy access."

Rico slid his finger in and slowly moved it out, bringing it to his mouth to get a taste of her.

"Damn you taste good."

Porsha could feel the hardness of his penis underneath her. Rico slid his fingers over her clit and down into her vagina and pulled it out. He continued to do this until Porsha couldn't take it anymore.

"Rico, please! I don't want to mess up my dress."

"Okay, I will let you slide for now."

Porsha moved back to her seat. She sat there in silence. She knew what she was doing can easily backfire on her. Porsha loved Jerome and had never stopped loving him, but now that Rico was in the picture, she knew she can easily fall for him. But, I can't he is the bad guy, she thought to herself.

"Roger, turn the car around and take us home. I'll have Janet prepare something for us." Rico directed as he glanced at Porsha.

"Is that okay?"

"Sure, that's fine."

Porsha knew what time it was. Her pussy started throbbing just thinking about his long, thick dick moving in and out of her.

They arrived at Rico's but before they headed upstairs, Rico went into the kitchen and spoke to Janet, the chef. Porsha stood at the entryway checking out the scenery. The kitchen was spacious. The island was made of glass, something she had never seen. The appliances were aluminum, which gave the kitchen a very expensive look. Porsha glanced over at Rico and Janet. She can't hear the conversation, but from the look on Janet's face, she was not too happy about what Rico asked her to do and she was letting him know that. As Rico made his way over to Porsha and kissed her on the lips, Janet was just standing there glaring at Porsha.

"What was that all about?" Porsha asked.

"Oh, don't worry about Janet. Let's just say she wished she were in your shoes.

"And you trust her to prepare dinner for us? Shit, she could poison us and no one will ever know it or suspect her."

Rico threw his head back and laughed. "Of course, she may be mad, not stupid."

Upstairs in the bedroom, the two can hardly contain themselves. Rico lay Porsha down on the bed. He slowly undressed, giving her plenty to look at. Once he was fully naked, he moved closer to the bed where she was and pulled her dress over her head and tossed it on the floor. He reached behind her and unsnapped her bra, letting the melons lay freely. Rico spread Porsha's legs and raised them in the air and climbed between them. He ran his tongue up and down her pussy from the front to the back of her ass. He stuck his tongue in and out of her asshole giving her a feeling that she'd never felt before. Once he sees her reaction to it, he made his way back to her nub and licked and sucked it until it becomes hard.

Rico climbed on top of her where he palmed her breast with one hand while taking the other breast in his mouth, turning her on even more. Porsha pulled Rico's body closer to her where she placed his penis between her breast as she pushed them together as tight as she could, instructing him to move his dick in and out of her breasts. As he began to do this, she licked his penis as he stroked her breasts, giving him a feeling he had never felt and to him, this was out of this world.

"Oh shit, that's it. Lick this dick." Rico moaned.

Porsha moved Rico off of her. As he lay on his back, Porsha raised his legs up in the air and climbed between his legs and licked the head of his penis while playing with his balls. She continued down to his ass and slid her tongue in and out as he had done her. She replaced her tongue with two fingers and began to slowly move in and out while moving up to place his penis back into her mouth. This feeling had caused Rico to lose it completely. Trying so hard to regain some self-control, Rico grabbed a hold of Porsha's head

"Baby, you are killing me softly. I have never been fucked in my ass before, but I have to say, it's a feeling I have never felt before and will never forget." Rico was trying to catch his breath.

Porsha continued fucking him in his ass and sucking his dick so good that when he came, it was the best orgasm that he had ever experienced. His entire body shook from the explosion.

Rico lay there for a good five minutes before he could move. Rico looked over at Porsha. "I'm sorry that you didn't get your nut off."

"There will be plenty of time for that," Porsha grinned slightly as she cuddled up to Rico.

Jerome, who was sitting outside the iron gates of Rico's home was unable to listen to the sex going on between the two. Jerome turned the receiver to silent mode. Jealousy was eating at him. He turned on the ignition and began to drive. Jerome had no clue where he was going he just knew he had to get away to clear his mind. Driving through the city streets of Indianapolis, Jerome took in the scenery trying to keep his mind off of Porsha. He turned on the radio and flicked through the stations. Unable to find something smooth to listen to, he reached for one of his favorite CD's and popped it in. One of Tiggy's songs, "Closer," echoed through the car. Forty- five minutes later, Jerome ended up at Jason's condo. He sat out front thinking about how stupid he had been acting lately. Of all people, I should know how addicting her sex game was, and I let myself get caught up in her web again.

Chapter Twenty-One

Caught Slipping

Inside the condo, Natalie and Mrs. Lee were making dinner when Mrs. Lee peeked out the front window and sees the black viper.
It looked like the same car that Derrick had asked her about. Panic began to set in, and she quickly called James.

"Calm down you are in good hands. You have no reason to be alarmed the person in the black viper is on our side." James reassured her.
Jerome's cell phone rang.

"Man, what are you trying to do! Lee spotted you in the front of the condo and phoned me!"

"I am so fucked up in the head right now. I don't know if I'm coming or going."
James puts Jerome on speaker so that John could listen in.

"Jerome, what's going on?"

"It's Porsha. She is getting in my head again. Right now she's with Rico fucking his brains out."

"Jerome, you need to snap out of it man. We have a job to do. There's no time for you to fall back in love with Porsha. Leave it alone, man." James demanded.

"You need to head back to the cabin," John said. "Enough is enough. What about your wife? If she finds out that you're cheating on her, she'll be devastated."

"I know, I know."
Jerome continued to sit after his conversation with the guys. He knew he had better listen or he could end up losing everything. He decided that they were right and that he should head to the cabin as soon as possible. Jerome was headed back to the hotel with his mind in a whirlwind. He pulled into the parking garage and drove to the fifth level. He was so consumed in his thoughts that he didn't see the white van following closely behind him until it was upon him. Jerome pulled into a spot and watched as the van passed him. He got out of his car and walked around to his trunk. Out of the corner of his eye,

he sees a shadow so he ducked down on the side of a car. Jerome stopped, pulled out his gun and looked around the parking garage for an exit. Thank God for a group of business men walking towards the elevators. Jerome quickly caught up with the group and board the elevator with them.

Jerome entered his hotel room and immediately slid the latch in place and propped a chair up against his the door. He dialed James and John.

"Hey... I think I've been made."

"What! Now you know you should have stayed your ass here, but no, you had to follow the pussy."

"Stay put we're on our way," James broke-in, breaking up John's tirade. Jerome didn't know that while he was spying on Rico and Porsha he was being watched by some of Rico's men. They hadn't figured out who he was but they knew he was the same guy from the scene at the house with Derrick.

Jerome made himself comfortable as he waited for his buddy's arrival. Hours later, Jerome walked out of the bathroom and glanced out his window. The city was lit- up and the view was astonishing. Knock, knock. Jerome turned to look in the direction of the door he pulled his gun out and walked over to the door. He looked through the peephole but the person on the other side had it covered up with their finger.

Jerome moved his ear to the door and listened for any sounds. "Stop playing, John... you're probably going to get us shot," James said.

"Oh, so he wants to play," Jerome said to himself.

Jerome quietly slid the latch from the door. He removed the chair and with one swift movement he snatched the door open and pointed his gun at John's face.

"Whoa! It's me, man!"

Jerome laughed as he pulled John inside.

"See, that's what your ass get, always playing around."

"At least I'm not chasing some woman."

Jerome gave John a stare that said don't go there.

As the three men made their way to the fifth-floor parking garage they found a man sitting on top of Jerome's car.

"What the fuck is your problem, sitting your ass on top of my baby," Jerome yelled as he pulled his gun out from his waist.

"Hold up, I mean you no harm. I'm sorry for sitting on your car, but I wanted to make sure I didn't miss you coming out. My name is Tommy, I work for Rico Lorenz. I know you're familiar with him. Ricky Carter was a friend of mine. I know what you guys are trying to do and I want to help you take this mother-fucker down."

"How do we know we can trust you and that this is not a setup? How do we know you're not the one who snitched on Ricky?"

"You don't, and I can't prove anything to you. All you have is my word, but what I can tell you when Rico is planning the biggest drug deal that has ever hit Indianapolis is going down... and where." Jerome looked at the man thoughtfully and said to James and John.

"I think we need to go somewhere, sit down, and hear the guy out. Let's go up to my room."

It was round two for Rico and Porsha. Porsha lays on her back as Rico licked her body down until he came to her pussy. He opened the folds of her pussy and began to lick her clit. He moved down to her vagina and inserted his tongue moving in and out and then moved up to her clit. He continued this movement until Porsha demanded that he enter her. Rico slowly inserted his dick into her ass.

"Oh my God! No Rico, no!"

"Calm down and relax. I promise it will only hurt for a minute."
Rico moved his dick in and out of her ass a little more until it was completely in. He moved in and out slowly. When he sees that she was calm he began to move a little faster.

"Oh shit, this is good!" Rico groaned.
Porsha began to please herself with her hand. The feeling of Rico's dick fucking her in the ass and her rubbing her clit felt so damn good that she bit down on her lip causing it to bleed.

"Oh Rico baby, fuck me harder! I said fuck me harder!"
Rico began to fuck her harder and harder until he collapsed on top of her.

"That was so damn good." He whispered in her ear.

Chapter Twenty-Two

Addicted to the sex

Sitting in the bedroom glancing out the window, Porsha felt bad. How could I help set-up a man who has treated her with the utmost respect, and it didn't help that he was a good fuck.

I can't do this. I have got to get a hold of Jerome to let him know that I am backing out.

"A penny for your thoughts," Rico said as he walked over to Porsha.

Porsha looked up and laughed.

"I am so happy being here with you right now." She smiled as she stood in front of Rico. She reached up and wrapped her arms around his neck, "No one has ever made me this happy."

"Oh, but it gets better."

Rico, there's something I need to tell you. Once you hear what I have to say, you may not want me around."

Just as she was about to tell Rico the real reason she was there, there was a knock at the door.

"Come on in, Janet."

Janet came in with their dinner. She moved further into the room and began moving the trays of food onto the table.

"Will there be anything else, Mr. Lorenz?" Janet asked, trying to avoid looking at Porsha. The smell of sex in the room infuriates her more.

"No, that will be all Janet."

"Let's talk as we eat dinner."

Rico guided Porsha to the table. He pulled out her chair and walked around the table to take his seat.

"This smells delicious."

"Believe me, it is. It's my favorite and since Janet is an excellent cook, I know you will enjoy it."

"What is all this?"

"We have shrimp and Chicken fried rice with egg rolls. Stuffed pepper steak and shrimp egg- foo- young.

"Oh my God, can we eat all of this?"

"Not all at once silly. We eat a little now and a little later."

After dinner, Porsha decided she had to tell Rico about Jerome. She didn't want to see anything bad happen to him.

"Rico we need to talk."

"Okay, let's have a seat outside on the balcony."

The two moved outside. The view and the surroundings were so peaceful. The tall trees that surround the house gave the home a scary, but calm and relaxing look and feel. The lawn was cut low at a diagonal angle, making everything look completely in place. She could see herself living here with Rico. Porsha sat down and took another sip of wine, she felt so at ease and so relaxed.

"You know, I could get used to this type of life."

Rico sat back and listen as he studied her.

Porsha paused; then plunged in. "Meeting you in the club that night was no accident. I was there on a mission and that mission was to meet you. I was brought in by some people that I had worked with many years ago to take down a drug dealer. I was called in about three weeks ago to assist them in taking down the largest drug dealer in Indianapolis, but the one thing that they didn't count on was me falling for the guy."

Rico rose from his chair and stood looking out over the balcony.

"So you're telling me that you're working for someone that wants to take me down. Do you know what I do to people who cross me?" Rico asked, turning his back to look at her.

"I'm not trying to cross you. That's why I am telling you this now," Porsha replied nervously beginning to feel uncomfortable.

"Who are these people?"

"They're undercover agents. They've been working hard for years to take you and your family down. You had a couple of undercover agents on your team, but you took them out."

"And I am supposed to believe you? Why would I?"

"Because I'm telling you the truth. I can't help them take you down because I'm falling in love with you."

"What? Are you serious? Don't you mean you're lusting after me because I'm damn sure lusting after you? You've got the best pussy and head game that I have had in all my days of chasing skirts."

"Don't you believe in love at first sight?"

"Hell no, I don't believe in love at first sight."

"I know you're angry right now, but just think about it. I know you care for me and you can't deny it. I see it in your eyes when you look at me and trust me; it is not the look of lust."

"I want you to leave my home right now while you can."

"Rico, please don't do this. Don't do this to us."

"To me, bitch, there is no us. I have a wife remember?"

Rico walked back into the room and made a call to his driver.

"I want her out of here right now. Send Chase up to my room ASAP."

Rico yelled from inside the room, "My driver will take you back to the hotel. He's downstairs waiting for you so I suggest you leave while you can."

Porsha walked back into the room. She looked at Rico with tears in her eyes.

"Rico, please don't do this, I want to be with you."

Porsha reached up to grab a hold of his hand, but he jerked it away from her. Rico was hurt. He had fallen hard for Porsha, but he was disappointed with himself for letting his guard down which could have cost him his freedom or his life.

Back in Jerome's hotel, Tommy discussed the big drug deal that would go down in two days. The guys had reservations about Tommy and what he was saying. In no way could they afford to walk into a trap planned by Rico.

Jerome stepped out into the hallway of the hotel and phoned his supervisor with the news Tommy shared with them. His supervisor instructed Jerome to keep Tommy there until he and his team arrived at the hotel.

Chapter Twenty-Three

Putting the plan into action

Thirty minutes later, David, Jerome's sergeant arrived at the hotel. He interrogated Tommy for about forty- five minutes. The last thing that he wanted to do was to have his men put in harm's way. Once he and his men felt comfortable with what Tommy had told them, he would put a plan into action. He had two days to come up with a solid plan.

The men left Tommy in the sitting area while the DEA agents gathered in Jerome's bedroom.

An hour later, they emerged from the room and rejoined Tommy in the sitting area.

"Tommy, what I need for you to do is to go back to Rico's and act like nothing has happened and wait for my call or if things change, you should call me ASAP," Jerome instructed.

On Tommy's way out of Jerome's room, he ran into Porsha. The two of them stared at each other, not knowing what to say or what to do. Tommy moved passed Porsha and heads for the elevator. Fearing that she will call Rico and tell him that she saw him leaving Jerome's room, so he turned back around and heads for Jerome's room not sure if he should take care of Porsha or let Jerome know what just happened.

Tommy knocked twice on Jerome's door before he answered.

"We got a problem. There's a chick name Porsha that's been messing around with Rico who seen me a couple of times at his house. She just saw me coming out of your room and looked at me strangely. I can't go back to Rico's. What if she tells him that she saw me leaving your room?"

"No worries, my boy," Jerome reassured him as he patted Tommy on the back. "She's on our side."

Tommy looked puzzled.

"We sent her to get close to Rico to be our eyes and ears."

"Aw, okay."

Tommy was on his way back over to Rico's when his phone rings.

"What's up?"

"Where the hell are you?" Rico yelled.

"I'm on my way to your crib now."

Tommy heard the click and then the dial tone.

"That's why I am setting your stupid ass up. I'm so sick of your bullshit." Tommy grumbled .

Porsha sat in her room debating whether or not she should phone Rico to tell him that she saw Tommy leaving Jerome's room.

"What am I doing? I can't believe I'm trying to help the bad guy," she said out loud.

Porsha decided to come clean with Jerome. She opened the door to her hotel room just as David and his team were walking out of Jerome's room. David had no idea that John had brought Porsha in on the case. David looked back at Jerome. "I know this is not what I'm thinking?"

John spoke up. "I took it upon myself to bring Porsha in to get close to Rico. She's the only person that could have done that."

"What, are you out of your fucking mind? Do you know she is not to be trusted anymore? She's the reason that my partner was murdered a couple of years ago! She turned against him while she was working undercover with him!"

"That was never proven," John replied coolly.

"I don't give a rats- ass if it was proven or not. I know in my heart that she is the reason he's not here today. I know it and she knows it." Porsha held her head down. She knew what he's saying was true. Again she crossed the line and put her team at risk.

"I'm sorry, John. David is right; just as I've done today. I confessed my intentions to the enemy."

Jerome moved in on Porsha. "You stupid bitch!" He roared as he reached for her. John grabbed a hold of Jerome before he could get his claws on her.

"I should ring your neck!"

"I'm sorry guys, this line of work is not for me anymore. Before anyone else dies or gets hurt, I am turning in my badge today." Porsha looked at Jerome, "I am sorry Jerome but Rico knows all about what you're planning. He's holding a meeting as we speak."

"Porsha, how could you do this to us? We trusted you. You put our team at risk." John said, shaking his head.

Porsha reached into her purse and pulled out her badge and her gun.

"David, can you turn this in for me."
David snatched the gun and the badge from Porsha. He looked at her not with hatred, but with a sympathetic look.
He had come across cases where people undercover fall for the bad guys. He knew how easy it was to get attracted to people with power and money.

"How much does Rico know Porsha?" James asked.

"He knows that I was working undercover to be your eyes and ears. I didn't find anything out, so I take it that's why he allowed me to walk away. Why was Tommy here?"
The men look at each other. "Porsha you didn't, tell me you didn't."

"I didn't what?"

"Tell me you didn't call Rico and tell him about Tommy," Jerome's eyes were narrow.

"No, I didn't and I won't. I promise."

Chapter Twenty-Four

A change of plans

The men regrouped for the second time in Jerome's room.

"I don't trust Porsha as far as I can see her."

"For all we know, we could be walking straight into a trap," James agreed.

"I say we keep still and wait until we talk with Tommy. If Tommy doesn't sound right, then we'll know something's up." David added.

Later that evening Jerome, John and James sat in the hotel's restaurant having dinner when Porsha walked in. She spied the men as soon as she walked in. Porsha heads in their direction.

"Can I join you guys?"

Jerome never looked up.

"Sure, why not," John shrugged.

"How could you turn on us like this?" Jerome asked, unable to hold it in.

"Jerome, I'm so sorry. I now know that I have a weakness when it comes to men--- sexy men that is."

"When are you heading to Cincinnati?" John asked.

"I'm leaving later tonight. I want to apologize to you guys before I leave. You put your trust in me and I turned against you. I never thought about how I put your lives in danger and for that, I am very sorry."

There was silence at the table. Jerome was past furious and James didn't expect anything different from Porsha because he never trusted her from the beginning. John felt bad. He felt like this was his fault for bringing her in.

Once Jerome was finished with his meal, he paid his bill and headed up to his room. He was unable to be near Porsha anymore without wanting to choke the shit out of her. He had put his trust in her and it backfired on him.

John and James checked into the hotel earlier that day after speaking with Tommy. They knew there was no reason to head back to the cabin with the news they've heard. The men finished their dinner and headed for their rooms, leaving Porsha to finish her dinner alone.

An hour later, Porsha checked her room for a second time just to make sure she didn't leave anything behind. She decided to leave Indiana and go live in Cincinnati with her mom. As she left the room, she glanced up at Jerome's door. She slowly made her way past his door, but stopped, turned back around and stood in front of his door. She stood there a few seconds, debating whether she should knock and or just leave.

On the third knock, Porsha decided to head out and leave things the way they were between Jerome and her and all of the memories they shared. Jerome stood on the other side of the door. He was pissed and a little hurt that Porsha would betray him and his men like she did. But there's one thing about Jerome… once you betray him, you will never get the opportunity to betray him again. Porsha gave up. She knew Jerome was in there. She made her way to the elevator. She couldn't blame him for not answering the door. She was not sure she would answer the door if the shoe were on the other foot. Porsha checked out of the hotel. She waited out front for the valet attendant to bring her car around. Minutes later she exited the hotel parking lot and headed for Cincinnati without ever looking back.

The next morning, Jerome got a text from Tommy.

"The deal is going down today at 1pm at the Northeast warehouse on Mass Ave."

"Oh fuck," Jerome called a meeting with the guys.

"The meeting is going down sooner than we expected. I haven't been able to get a hold of David and the rest of the gang, but I did leave David a text message.

"I want to be in that area at least two hours before anyone arrives. I say we go now to scope out the place."

"Let's go. We can take my car." James said.

The guy's head for the elevator to the parking garage and head for James' 2013 Black Buick LaCrosse.

"Man, this car still smells brand new why don't you drive this more often?" John asked.

119

James glanced at John. I like to save this for special occasions, but since we have been hiding out, there haven't been any special occasions."

As they get closer to the building, John asked, "Is that it?"

"This is the address that Tommy gave me."

"I hope this is not a setup," James remarked.

"That's why we are here early. Arriving early will give us extra time to check out the place." Jerome said.

The three found a close place to ditch the car and head toward the building on foot.

"Something just doesn't feel right to me," Jerome said nervously.

"Has David returned your call or responded to your text message?" John asked.

"No, not yet. That's not like David either."

As the men come upon the building they heard voices coming from the front of the building. They quietly move toward the sound.

"You guys stay here and let me peep out to see who's in front," Jerome whispered.

Jerome peeked around the building. He was confused at what he sees. He moved back to the men, "This is a set-up. Let's get out of here."

The men took off running in the direction of the car. Once they were inside, Jerome told them, "You're not going to believe who was there talking with Rico and his men."

Chapter Twenty-Five

Go with your gut feeling

"**Who** did you see talking to Rico and his goons?" James continued to question Jerome.

"David and two of his men were there, talking to Rico. David was talking about us. I heard him mention our names and Tommy's. I heard Rico tell David that Porsha came clean with him and that he was about to blow her head off but couldn't find it in his heart to hurt a woman."

"Aw hell no, you can't trust anyone these days."

"I need to contact Tommy to see where he is and if he's okay, but after seeing David talking to Rico and his men, God only knows what has happened to him," Jerome said.

As they drove away from the area, Jerome called Tommy but it went straight to his voice- mail. Jerome sent him a text and waited for a response.

Twenty- five minutes later, Tommy responded back with a text "SET-UP!!!"

"I knew it. I knew something didn't seem right. Jerome grumbled and asked James to pull over. Jerome responded back to Tommy.

"Where are you? Are you okay?"

Tommy responded back. "Yes, I am okay. I'm getting out of town while I can."

"Text me once you get where you are going," Jerome replied.

"Thank God he is okay."

"I know he's probably scared shitless," James said quietly.

"So what are we going to do now?" John asked.

"We're going to do what we should have done in the beginning. I'm contacting my contact in internal affairs."

Jerome made the call and was on the phone with his contact when out of nowhere a truck rear-ended James' car.

"What the hell, oh hell naw! That son of a bitch just fucked up my car." James yelled.

Another truck appeared out of nowhere on the passenger side and slammed into the side of the car where Jerome was seated.

"You okay?" James yelled.

"Yes, I'm fine! Get us the hell away from these mother-fuckers!" Jerome shouted.

Jerome was still on the phone with internal affairs, telling his contact what was happening.

"Where are you guys?"

"We are approaching the downtown area. We are heading west to College Avenue."

"If you can get to College Avenue I can have back up waiting there for you guys."

"Get us to College Avenue ASAP," Jerome said quickly.

The two trucks were still on their tail and continued to rear end James when one of the passengers from the truck on the right started shooting.

James began to swerve in and out of traffic trying to avoid the bullets.

"Duck down John," James grunted." Just as John ducked down a bullet hit the back window and it shattered it into pieces. James made a quick right trying to lose the perpetrators, but unfortunately, they were still on his tail.

"You okay John?" Jerome asked, his eyes darted to the trucks following.

"Yeah, damn that was close."

"College should be coming up shortly," Jerome said pointing.

Just as James made a quick left onto College Avenue, several police cars greeted them. One of the truck rear- ended him again. James barely made it through the barricade when the other police cars close the gap as the trucks try to pass. They were trapped in a circle surrounded by police officers.

The police officers rushed out of their cars with their weapons drawn. "Get out of the truck with your hands in the air!" The police shouted as they surrounded the truck. The men get out with their hands in the air. The police confiscated their weapons out of the truck while the other police officers frisked the men down before handcuffing them.

Back at the station, Jerome was in the office of internal affairs along with James and John.

"We have captured four of Rico's men. We're on the search for Rico and another man."

"What about David and his men?" Jerome asked.

"We brought them in about ten minutes ago. They're being held in the interrogation room."

After several hours of being interrogated, David and his men decided to talk.

"The deal is going down tomorrow, but if I'm not there, Rico may become suspicious."
Eddie of Internal Affair looked evenly at the man. "Too damn bad. You will text Rico tomorrow to let him know you're going to be late and to go ahead without you."
David looked puzzled as he eyed Eddie.

"Did you think I was going to let you show up to the meeting? I was born at night, but not last night." Eddie said sarcastically.
Jerome and his men sat in Eddie's office going over plans to bust Rico and his men tomorrow.

"I hope this works," Jerome said.

"I know you're not trusting of people right now, but believe me, we're on the same side."

"I hope so," Jerome responded as he eyed Eddie.

"So far, have I let you down? Who came to your rescue today?"

"Hell, that doesn't mean anything to me right now. You could be setting us up for the something else."

"Jerome, all I am asking is that you trust me. If I prove you wrong then I will admit to it, but don't count me out when I haven't done anything for you not to trust me."

"I know, but if things don't seem right tomorrow, I'm getting myself and my men out as soon as possible."

"I wouldn't expect anything less from you."

"I agree. If things don't feel right, get out… but let us know so we can get out as well."

"What do you mean?"

"Did you think I was sending you guys in alone?"

"Well, yes."

"I keep trying to tell you, we are on the same side, the same team Jerome."

Eddie and Jerome shook hands and Jerome and his men head back to
the hotel for a good night's sleep before their big day.
Jerome looked at the other two men. "I don't know about you guys,
but I need a stiff drink before I head to my room."

"That sounds good to me," John agreed.

"What about you James? Are you up for it?"

"No, I will pass. I'll see you guys in the morning and don't stay
down here too late."

"Okay, Dad." Jerome said, grinning as he shook his head at James.
He had no clue as to how true this was going to be.
The men sat and talked about the day's events when John brought up
Porsha.

"Jerome, how do you feel about Porsha now that she crossed us?"

"I hate her guts. We all could have been killed behind her mess. I
don't understand her and did you hear what David said about his
partner being murdered because of her?"

"Yeah, but after what he did, I'm not sure I trust anything that
comes out of his mouth."

James heads up to his room to take a shower. As he entered his room,
an overwhelming feeling rushed over him. His heart started to beat
rapidly and the urge to be with Lee consumed him. James shook his
head as if he was trying to shake this feeling off, but little did he
know that Lee will play a very important role in his life… whether he
wanted to believe it or not.
James stood under the shower as the hot water ran down his sore body
from the day's events. He thought back to the time at the cabin when
Lee was sleeping downstairs and he came down to check on her. The
feeling that came over him when he saw her breast spilling out of her
blouse and her shapely- toned legs. He had always felt something
special for Lee, but he thought it was because she was his best
friend's mom, but now he knew different. Every day since the cabin,
his feelings have grown stronger for her and no matter how much he
tried to deny it, something lets him know otherwise. What am I going
to do? He thought to himself. There was no way he could act on his
feelings unless she felt the same way he did.
James stepped out of the shower and grabbed a towel. He had got to
get this off my chest right now. James grabbed his phone and dialed
the number. Lee picked up on the third ring.

"Hello James, how are you?" Lee asked in her sexiest voice. Thrown off by the way Lee sounded, James was stunned. "I am doing well, Lee. You were on my mind, so I wanted to call and check on you."

"Is that all you wanted?" Lee asked as she giggled like a schoolgirl.

Again, he was stunned. "Can we talk about some things that have been on my mind once our mission is over?"

"Sure… why not."

"I'll call you in a couple of hours okay?"

"Talk to you then."

Lee ended the call, but James was still holding the phone to his ear. His heart just dropped to his stomach… at least that's how it felt. A stirring in his groin let him know he had better get a hold of himself when it came to Lee.

Chapter Twenty-Six

The morning of

Jerome awoke just as the sun began to rise. He threw the covers over his head to block the morning sun- rays shining through the blinds. He continued to lay there. He was not ready to start his day just yet. His body was begging for more sleep, but his mind knew it was time to get the day started.

Jerome dragged his body out of the bed and into the bathroom where he stood in front of the sink, glancing at himself in the mirror.

"Man, I look tired," He said to himself as he grabbed his toothbrush and toothpaste.

Thirty minutes later, Jerome was dressed and was sitting on the side of his bed when his phone vibrated. He looked at the number, but didn't recognize it. He started to ignore it and let it go to voice mail, but something told him to answer it.

"Hello… Hello?"

"Jerome, this is Tommy. The dude that was in your hotel room the other day is dirty. He told Rico that you were onto him."

"I know, but you don't have to worry about him anymore, we have him in custody."

"But Rico knew I had been talking to you. The word on the street is that he wants me dead."

"I figured as much. Just stay out of sight until later tonight. Once things are clear, I will contact you. Where are you staying, if you don't mind me asking?"

"I'm at a friend's house outside of Indianapolis."

"Okay, just be careful and I will hit you up later."

Jerome ended the call and phoned John.

"John, I just got off the phone with Tommy.

He's good, but he said the word out on the street is that he has a price on his head. I told him to stay low and that I would contact him later once Rico and the others are in custody."

"Well, that's good. I would hate to have his death on our hands because he tried to help us out," John said.

"I know what you mean. I need to call and tell James what's going on. Have you talked to him this morning?"

"No, not yet."

"Okay, let me call him and keep him in the loop."

After Jerome got off the phone with James, they agreed to meet downstairs for breakfast. On his way down, James stopped at John's room to tell him about breakfast. Walking down the hall to the elevator, there was an eerie feeling that ran down Jerome's spine. He turned around to check out his surroundings. The halls were quiet, not a person in sight. He continued his walk to the elevator.

As Jerome rode down Jerome's phone rang, but this time he recognized the number.

"Not this time Porsha I am through with you."

Jerome ignored the call as he exited the elevator. He continued walking to the restaurant to meet the boys. Once he entered, his phone rang again, this time it was Eddie calling.

"What's good, Eddie?"

"Hey Jerome, is John and James with you?"

"Yeah, what's up?'

"I had David call Rico this morning. The deal is still going down, but the time has changed from one to ten am. I need you guy's downtown in about an hour."

"Okay, we are going to grab some breakfast and we'll head your way afterward."

"Cool"

Jerome made his way to where he sees James and John.

"Hey, I just got off the phone with Eddie. He wants us to meet him downtown in an hour. He said David called Rico this morning and the deal is going down at ten instead of one. I told him we were getting breakfast and afterward, we would meet him downtown."

The men were sitting at the table waiting for their food when John's phone rings. John looked at the number and looked up at Jerome.

"Don't tell me… its Porsha calling."

"How did you know?"

"She called me earlier and I let it go to voice mail."

"So she can't get to you so she reaches out to John," James said as he shook his head.

"Yep, that about sums it up, the woman is crazy. I should have never got involved with her."

"Why is she trying so hard to reach you?" John asked.

"I have no idea and I don't care why. She can rot in hell as far as I'm concerned."

The entire time, James mind was going in circles. He could only hope Jerome was through with her because he would hate for him to lose his wife over the likes of Porsha.

After breakfast, the men head for town. Jerome took his car while James and John rode together in John's car. After yesterday's event, James had to put his car in the shop.

After the meeting with Eddie, the men head out. The game was on and they were so ready to get this day over. Jerome had been waiting for this day for so long. It seemed surreal that it was going down this morning.

The men, along with several of Eddie's men were hiding out in the warehouse waiting for Rico, his men and his connections from Miami to arrive. They waited for thirty minutes, but still, no one had arrived.

"Are you sure David told you the truth? Right now, I don't trust him as far as I can throw him." Jerome remarked.

Just then, they heard a car pull up. It was a black town car. It looked just like Rico's car. Rico's driver got out and walked to the back of the car and opened the trunk. He pulled out a large silver case and set it on the ground. He then shut the trunk and went to the back passenger door and opened the car door. Rico's goon got out. Rico was the last to step out of the car. When Rico got out, he looked around at his surroundings and motioned for the driver to open the door of the warehouse. The driver, along with one of Rico's men eased inside to check it out before Rico went in. Just as Rico entered, another car pulled up. This time it was a black hummer. The driver and the passenger hopped out of the hummer and went to the back and opened each door. Two large, Italian men emerged from the back of the Hummer and made their way inside the warehouse.

Chapter Twenty-Seven

The Takedown

The men gathered at the table stationed in the middle of the warehouse. Roger, Rico's driver lay the suitcase on the table while the two Italian men opened their suitcases filled with drugs. The street value of the drugs was valued at 4.5 million dollars.

The man asked Rico "Do I need to count this or can I trust you?"

"If it will make you sleep better tonight, go ahead and count it," Rico replied coolly.

Just as he was about to count the money, Eddie came out of nowhere. "I want you all too slowly move away from the table and put your hands in the air."

The men looked in his direction and one by one the men on his team made their presence known. Jerome walked over to Rico.

"You know, I've been waiting for this for a long time. I'm going to see to it that you don't see the outside for as long as you live." Rico smiled. "So it's true what I've heard about you?"

Jerome ignored Rico and began to search Rico before putting him into handcuffs. Within minutes all of the men have been captured.

This seemed too easy, Jerome thought. He hesitated a little before heading outside with Rico. Just as he moved further to the door, they all turn to the sound of a loud crash. A big truck came crashing through the back wall and about ten men jump out with guns in their hands. Rico looked at Jerome and smiled, "Ha ha, mother-fucker, now the jokes on you. Take these damn cuffs off me before you make me mad. Killing you a second time is going to be my pleasure."

The men gathered Eddie and his crew up. They began to tie each man's hands behind them and moved them to the center of the room. They placed them sitting in a circle so they could watch each other as gasoline was being poured all around them.

"You can sit here and watch as each one of you die!" one of the men shouted before heading out.

The last guy out of the warehouse was the one who lit the fire that burned a circle around the men. In an instant, the flames became so high that you couldn't see the men anymore. The men began to cough as they struggled to get loose. The smoke began to burn at their eyes so they were forced to work with their eyes closed trying to get loose. You couldn't see anything, so no one saw Tommy when he sneaked in from the back where the truck had crashed through the wall. Tommy managed to get inside the circle and untied Jerome's hands. Jerome and Tommy worked fast to untie the others and rushed out the back way and jump into the car Tommy had arrived in. Their eyes and throat burned from the smoke. They sat in the back seat of the truck coughing as Eddie got on the phone and called for backup as Tommy zeroed in on the hummer, the truck, and the black town car. He made sure he stayed his distance until backup arrived.

Rico sat in the back seat of his town car with a smirk on his face. He thought he had killed the perpetrator for the second time. Ten minutes into his ride, his head jerked forward as the car rear- ended his car. Eddie had given Tommy the okay to rear end the car seeing that their backup had arrived. Quickly, the Hummer, truck and town car was surrounded by the FEDS. There was no way they were going to get out of this without being arrested.

Downtown at the police station, Jerome was thrilled. He was thrilled that he had accomplished his goal of taking Rico and his men down. He was also thrilled that he could go home to his wife and his mom. He could not wait to get back to his normal life. He wanted to finish his last class at law school and take the bar exam. Jerome, James, and John had plans of opening up their own law firm, but working on this case for such a long time had put a damper on their dreams; a dream they could now live.

"You guys ready to go home with me so I can see my wife and my mom?"

"Man, I can't wait to see the look on their face," John agreed.

"Well, what the hell are we waiting for?" James said.

The men all shake Eddie's hand and rushed out of the building to their cars. Jerome drove his car while John and James ride together.

As the men pulled up in front of the house, Jerome sat there anxious, excited and nervous at the same time. How was his wife going to feel about him? Would she forgive him for being away or will she be upset and angry with him? These were the questions that filled his head.

"Are you going to just sit here?" John asked as he walked over to Jerome's car.

Jerome got out and made his way up the walkway as John and James followed behind. Jerome had no idea that James was just as excited as he was to see Lee. Jerome pulled his key out and inserted it into the lock. He turned the knob slowly and pushed the door open. What he saw stopped him in his tracks. His wife was standing there looking at a picture of them on their wedding day with tears in her eyes. Jerome walked up behind her and wrapped his arms around her. She turned at the feel of his embrace and stared at him. Jerome brushed his lips across hers as she continued to stare at him like she had just seen a ghost.

"Jason, is that you Jason?" Natalie asked as she looked him in the eyes.

"Yes Nat, it is me. It's your husband."

Just then Mrs. Lee walked in the room. She glanced up at Jerome and does a double-take. "Jason Jerome!" She yelled as she rushed to his side.

Jerome hugged his mom and kissed her on her cheek.

"Oh my God, what is going on here?" She asked.

Natalie was in shock. She stood there glued to the floor. She tried to move, but her feet will not move. James and John move further into the room and stood by Natalie. They could tell she had not digested seeing Jason. James wrapped his arms around her as she began to cry out loud.

"Oh my God, oh my God, oh my God, I can't believe it's you, Jason!"

Jason grabbed a hold of Natalie and walked her to the couch where they sat. He began to tell her everything from the beginning.

"Well, Natalie, you continued to say you knew he wasn't dead. I was beginning to think you were losing your mind, but I guess you knew more than what I did."

"I can't believe you did this to us."

"There's something else I need to tell you. Mrs. Lee is not just my housekeeper, she's my mom. I had to keep her identity a secret so that she would be safe. Do you know what Derrick would have done if he knew she was my mom?"

"Are they any more secrets, Jason?"

"No, there are no more secrets. Just know I did this for your safety. I could not have Rico and his men do anything to you. Trust me they could care less about hurting women. Oh, I guess there is one more secret. James, John and I were working undercover we are part of the DEA team. We've been undercover for years and we will be finishing up with our law degree and taking the bar exam, and opening up our own law firm soon."

"What? You have got to be kidding me. I feel like I'm married to a stranger. I know nothing about you!"

"I'm telling you all you need to know now."

"Now what about in the beginning, why didn't you feel you could tell me this then and still keep me safe?"

"I didn't feel that I could keep you safe so I decided to keep you in the dark. I hope you can forgive me?"

"I don't know. I feel like our marriage was a lie," Natalie said quietly as she got up and walked over to the window.

"Is this your getaway condo? Is this where you bring your women to keep me from finding out about them?"

"Natalie, I had this condo before we even started dating. This was my place away from home. I came here when I needed to clear my mind; to get away from the real world."
As Jason and Natalie talk, James approached Lee. "Hey, how are you?"

"I'm fine now that I have my son back. How are you?" Lee asked as she touched James' hand. "I see you're walking a little stiff there."

"We had a little incident yesterday in my car so I'm a little sore. Can we take a walk outside and talk if you don't mind?" James asked.

"Sure, let me grab my jacket."
James felt a little uneasy about asking Lee to step outside with him. He didn't want to draw any attention to them... especially not Jason's attention.
Lee came back with her Jacket in hand and escaped through the side door and signaled for James to go through the front door. James headed out and met up with Lee at the end of the driveway.

"I feel like a teenager, sneaking out of the house to meet the bad boy in the neighborhood."
James laughed. "I guess you have some experience with that?"
Lee softly nudged James in the side. "Whatever, I'm just saying."

"What are we doing, Lee? I know you feel some kind of way as I do." James said seriously as he stopped to face her.

'You tell me. I've noticed lately that when I'm around you, I feel a certain way, and it's not a feeling that I get when I'm around John."

"Okay, so what are we going to do about these feelings we have for each other?" James asked as he wrapped his arms around Lee bringing her closer to him. The feel of his strong arms wrapped around her did all kinds of things to her. Lee looked up at James and his eyes captivated her. The gray- eyed man had captured part of her heart and he didn't even know it. Lee had always felt something for James, but always downplayed it... but now, she was ready to let him in and let the world know how she felt.

Chapter Twenty-Eight

What you do in the dark will come to light

Natalie, Jason, and Mrs. Lee move back into their home.

"Oh, it feels so good to be back home!" Mrs. Lee told Natalie. Natalie stood looking out of the kitchen window in a daze. She was still upset. She felt that she and Jason had been living a lie. She didn't know if she could trust him anymore. What if there was something else he hadn't told her? Would she be able to forgive him? Natalie wondered.

"Mrs. Lee, can I ask you a question?"

"Yes, sweetheart, what is it?"

"Do you think Jason was right in keeping all of this a secret from me?" she asked as she took a seat on the bench by the window.

"You know, I would have probably done things differently, but I believe Jason thought what he was doing was right at the time. You wanted Jason's death to be a dream. Now that he's here, enjoy him, because you know how quickly life events can take your loved ones from you. If you don't, you might end up regretting it. Trust me, I know."

"What do you mean I know'?"

Lee walked over where Natalie was and took a seat next to her.

"Natalie, I have found someone I truly believe I could fall in love with. I have known this person for a very long time and I have always felt something for this person, but I continued to deny it. Now I want the world to know, but I'm not sure how my son will feel about it. So I'm a little scared, but what I keep thinking is that I'm not getting any younger and the good Lord could call me home at any time. So I need to enjoy everything while I am here on earth. You feel me?"

"Yes, I do."

Later that night, Jason stepped out of the shower and entered the bedroom with a bath towel wrapped around his body. Natalie had forgotten how sexy her husband was. She lay there in bed as she watched him move his muscular body across the room. His six- pack and his hairy chest turned her on. But because she was still a little salty with him she turned over and ignored the heat running through her body. She thought about what Lee said earlier about how life's event can quickly take away the ones you love. She should know all too well about life's events, but her stubbornness kept her from enjoying the man she fell in love with years ago. Jason eased his nakedness in bed and scooted closer to Natalie. Natalie had her back turned toward him and pretended to be asleep. Jason began to plant kisses at the nape of her neck and moved down her back planting little kisses. He took his tongue and ran it up her spine until he reached her neck. The feel of his tongue running up her ignited a feeling that Natalie had not felt in a while. Natalie turned around to face Jason. The look in his dark brown eyes alone set her on fire, but his smile, white teeth, and facial features reminded her of why she fell in love with this man. Jason kissed her eyes, her nose and all around her lips. Natalie opened her mouth to let Jason in. He kissed her like there was no tomorrow and she matched his hungriness. Jason removed his mouth from her and moved down to her breasts. He took one of her nipples in his mouth, sucking and licking it until it became hard. Then he moved to the other one. He made his way down south of the border where he unfolded her lips until her clit was visible. He took his tongue and slowly moved it up and down slowly inserting it in and out of her until she could not take it anymore and exploded. Jason moved up her body until he reached her mouth. He stuck his tongue inside she sucked on it like a lollipop. Jason guided his penis to her treasure and slowly entered her. He moved in and out of her slowly at first and then faster, deeper and wilder.

"Oh, Jason baby, I've missed you so much."

"Then show me, baby, show me."

Jason rolled over bringing Natalie with him. She was now straddling him and taking him for a ride of his life. Natalie rose up slowly and then slams down on his penis. Natalie did this several times before Jerome held her by the waist as he grinds deeper inside of her and they both exploded together.

"Damn, baby you need to ride me like this all the time." Jerome pants as he rubbed his fingers across her breasts.

The next two weeks were wonderful for Natalie and Jason. Jason and his buddies, along with Tommy, testified against Rico and his men. Rico got twenty- five years to life for murder, attempted murder, drug possession and possession of cocaine with the attempt to distribute, and the list goes on. Tommy was given three years of probation for cooperating with the authorities and his testimony. The men finished law school and passed the bar exam. They were very excited about starting their own law firm. The men worked hard at finding the right location and with the help of a well-known Real Estate company called DH Realty, LLC, they helped make their dream a reality.

One month later, James and Lee have made it official; they were a couple, but unfortunately, no one else knew but the two of them. Lee continued to tell James that she would sit Jason down and tell him, but that day has yet to come.
It was Friday afternoon, the big day for Jason, James, and John. Tonight, they would be celebrating the opening of their new law firm called The J3 law firm. Natalie and Mrs. Lee were busy at work preparing for the grand opening party. Natalie was working with the caterers while Mrs. Lee was working with the party planner, making sure everything would be perfect for the special occasion tonight.
   "Jason baby, you look so delicious in your white tux. White is definitely your color."
   "Thank you, babe," Jason grinned as he kissed his wife on the lips. "You know, you look pretty good yourself in that tan form- fitting dress, showing all my shit." They both laughed.
   "If this wasn't such a special occasion, I would ask if we could forgo the party and just stay here and enjoy each other."
   "That sounds tempting." Natalie laughed lightly, but I doubt that James and John would understand."

James arrived at 8:30 to escort Lee to the party. No one had figured out why James was escorting Lee when she could have easily rode with Jason and Natalie. James showed up at the door with a bouquet of roses for Lee. Jason was thrown off, but Natalie kind of sensed something was going on with the two but didn't say anything just yet. James looked stunning in his gray Armani suit with a pink shirt: the gray set off the gray in his eyes. Lee was dressed in a salmon color

140

knit dress that clinged to her body, showing off her curves and her full breasts. James was amazed at how good she looked. He knew she was fine, but tonight, she took fine to a different level. He swore if Jason and Natalie weren't staring at them like they had three eyes, he would have taken her right where she was standing.

Chapter Twenty-Nine

The party pooper

Lee told Jason and Natalie that she was riding with James so they could be alone. This whole ordeal had put a strain on their marriage. She just hoped Natalie can find it in her heart to forgive and forget. In the meantime, Lee and James were still trying to hide their feelings from everyone, but tonight, Lee wanted to let him know exactly how she felt. She wanted to tell everyone because she was tired of keeping her feelings inside.

James and Lee arrived at the D'Amore on the 48th floor of the Chase Tower. They rode up the elevator with another couple who anyone could tell they were very much in love. Lee looked at James and at that moment the feelings that the two had for each other scared them. Neither one of them had ever felt such a connection with anyone. Lee moved to stand in front of James and leaned back against his chest. James wrapped his arms around her waist and bent his head to kiss her on her cheek. Lee turned to face James.

"You know, I could just stay here for the rest of the night with you. It wouldn't bother me one bit if I missed the party. James threw his back and laughed. "I don't think Jason would be too happy with me, keeping his mom from such a special night for the three of us."

"Yeah, you're right. I was just being selfish. Have I told you how proud I am of you?"

"Yes, but you can tell me again," James said as he smiled at the woman who made him forget his promise to himself not to get his feelings involved with her or any woman.

As the elevator doors opened, James and Lee were shocked to see John standing there. "Oh my God Lee said quietly as she moved away from James. John looked at the couple as if they have lost their damn minds, but James chuckled as he walked off the elevator with Lee's hand secured in his own. He found it pretty funny, actually.

"Close your mouth before something flies in," James whispered to John leaning over as he and Lee walked towards the entrance.

Ten minutes later, Natalie and Jason made their presence known. They were the last ones to arrive. Everyone began to applaud the couple.

"Oh my God Jason, I can't believe all of these people came out to celebrate with you guys."

"I know. It feels good to know so many people care."
Jason waved his hand at the guests and turned to his wife. He pulled her to him and kisses her on the cheek.

"Well, well… who do we have here?" Porsha said as she eyed Natalie up and down.
Jason stared at Porsha. "What are you doing here?" he grumbled as he plants himself in front of Natalie.

"I know you didn't think I would let you celebrate this special occasion without me, did you?"

"Jason, who is this?" Natalie asked.

"No one special," He said curtly as he guided Natalie to the other side of the room.
Porsha started to follow the couple, but James and John intercepted her before she had a chance to cause any problems for the couple.

"Now, you know you do not belong here." James' voice was like bitter honey as he grabbed a hold of Porsha's arm.
Porsha jerked away from James. "Get your fucking hands off me you fucking loser. Be a good boy and go play some damn where." Lee heard the conversation and began to get pissed. "Who is calling a loser?" Lee asked James.

"Let it go, babe," James replied low, his eyes not leaving Porsha. By the way Porsha was slurring her words, they could tell that she had consumed too much to drink.

"Porsha, why don't I call you a cab?"

"For what? The party has just started and now you're trying to get rid of me? I don't think so."

"Porsha, don't do this now." James eyes still had not left her for a second.

"What are you talking about, James? Why don't you want me to tell Jerome's wife that I'm pregnant with his child? Why should this child be a secret?"
James ran his hand across his face as he stood in front of Lee. He knew Porsha was nothing but trouble and tried to warn Jason, but

no… Jason wouldn't listen. I bet he will listen now. James thought to himself.

"What did you just say?" Lee asked as she stepped in front of James now.

Before Porsha had a chance to respond to Lee, James guided Porsha outside on the balcony.

"Porsha, why are you doing this? You know damn well you were fucking Rico as well. How can you be so sure this is Jason's baby?"

"I don't have to explain anything to you or John. Jerome knows this is his baby, and that's all that matters." Porsha slurred as she made her way back inside where she scanned the room for Jason.

"Jason, who is that woman?"

"I told you, nobody. Don't let that drunk cause us to not enjoy ourselves tonight. Can you do that for me?"

Natalie looked up at the man she loved more than life and smiled.

"I promise I won't let anything or anyone spoil this night for us. Jason grabbed a hold of Natalie's hand and guided her to the dance floor. He pulled her close to him and wrapped his arms around her waist as she wrapped her arms around his neck. Jason pulled her a little closer so she can feel the hardness in his pants. "I want you so bad I could take you right here where you stand."

"I can tell, or should I say I can feel," Natalie nuzzled his ear gently whispering." Just hold tight until we make it home."

John had been successful in keeping Porsha company so that she wouldn't ruin the night for Natalie and Jason, but just before the party ended, Porsha found Jason.

"There you are! We need to talk. Can we go somewhere private?" Porsha asked.

"What do you want with my husband?"

"Do you really want to know?" Porsha tittered.

"Porsha, we can go outside and talk. Honey, I'll be right back." Jason gave his wife's hand a reassuring squeeze and guided Porsha away from Natalie.

"What is your fucking problem?" Jason hissed as he grabbed a hold of Porsha's arm. "How dare you come here to start this bullshit?"

"Bullshit? It wasn't bullshit when I was fucking you in your ass, so why does it have to be bullshit now? Jason, all I want to do is to let you know I'm pregnant. I am pregnant with your child."
Natalie stood outside the door listening to the conversation between Porsha and Jason.

"What the fuck is going on? What does she mean she is pregnant with your child?" Natalie demanded as she burst through the doors allowing others at the party to hear the conversation.
Porsha staggered over to Natalie. "You heard right, honey. I'm carrying your husband's child. Ask him about the times we made love while he worked undercover and how I fucked him so damn good it had his head all messed up. Go ahead, and ask him."

"Jason, what is she talking about? Tell me this is not true?" Jason turned around and walked over to Natalie and grabbed her by the arms.

"We're out of here."

"No! We are not going anywhere until you tell me what the hell is going on."

"Can we talk about this at home?"

"No, we can't. I may not want you to come home after I hear what you have to say."

"Natalie, don't do this to us."

"Me? I'm not the one accused of having an affair and impregnating someone."

"I can explain. Let's just go home and we can sit down and talk about everything."
Jason guided Natalie outside to the car. The ride home was awkward for Jason. Natalie cried the entire ride home. Jason hated to see his wife so upset behind his lust. Jason pulled the car over on the side of the road. He grabbed Natalie's hand.

"Natalie, look at me! Listen, I did sleep with Porsha a couple of times while undercover, but I only did it to get back at her for how she treated me before I met you, but then things got out of hand. I did not intend to get her pregnant, nor do I want a relationship with her... I want you."
Natalie yelled as she hit Jason with her fist with a left and right hook, "Jason, if she has that bastard, I will divorce you so you damn well better make sure your bitch does not have that baby!"

Jason tried to block Natalie punches, but one hit caught him in the mouth. Infuriated, Jason got out of the car and started walking. He had never put his hands on a woman, but tonight he was so tempted to with Porsha tonight, and now with Natalie. Jason wiped his mouth as the blood ran down.

"Shit." He spat out as he noticed the blood on his white tux.

"Jason, Jason come back. I'm sorry, come back!" Natalie got behind the wheel and drove to where Jason was and blew the horn behind him. Jason turned back to look at Natalie. "What Natalie, what do you want? You already busted my lip; I got blood on my new tux."

"I'm sorry baby, get back in the car."
Jason got in on the passenger side and Natalie pulled off. They arrived home ten minutes later. Jason decided to sleep in one of the guest rooms until things cooled off between him and Natalie.

Meanwhile, Lee and James enjoyed themselves at the party. John had called a cab for Porsha and sent her to her hotel room.
John stood back and watched the interactions between James and Lee. The two seem a little more than just friends. When they were dancing they danced just a little too close for John's liking and if he didn't know any better, he would have sworn he saw James's hands on Lee's butt.

Chapter Thirty

The Day After

The next day Natalie awoke to the smell of coffee brewing bacon and eggs cooking and the sound of the morning news. This was what she was accustomed to, but today she didn't feel like her old self. There were so many things that have transpired within the last six months that she didn't know what to do or how to feel. Last night started out as the best night, but ended with her husband's mistress crashing their party with news that she was carrying his child. Natalie continued to lay in bed with the covers pulled up to her chest. She listened as the footsteps walked outside of her room back and forth as if someone was guarding her room.

"What the hell is going on?" She asked as she threw the covers across her bed and made her way to the bedroom door. As she opened the door, she was met with men moving furniture upstairs.

"What's going on?" She asked as Jason approached her.

"I'm having Lee's room moved up here and her new furniture is being delivered."

"Oh, I completely forgot about that, and just so you know, I meant what I said about your bitch having that baby. If that baby lives, you might as well marry the bitch." Natalie growled as she slammed the door shut.

Lee walked over to Jason. "You can't blame her, Jason. She thought you were dead. She mourned your death and then she finds out that you are alive, and now she has to deal with the fact that you cheated on her… and not only that, but you got that person pregnant. Give her some time to get over all of this."

"But she wants me to make sure Porsha doesn't have this baby, and if she does have it, she is threatening to divorce me. What can I do? I can't make Porsha abort the child. It is not that easy."

"I know, but you will just have to figure something out."

Later that evening, the three of them were sitting in the dining room having dinner when the doorbell rang.

"I'll get it," Natalie said, getting up. I need some air anyway."
Natalie made her way to the front door when she sees a female.
Natalie's instincts kicked in as she snatched the door open.

"What the hell do you want?"

"Oh my, is Jason here? I'm going to the doctor tomorrow and I
wanted to know if Jason wanted to come with me since he's the
baby's father."

"Bitch, you got some nerve bringing your ratchet- ass over to my
home. If you know what's good for you, you will take your stupid
ass somewhere else before I beat the black off of you."

"Jason!" Porsha yelled loud enough for Jason to hear her and tried
to move inside the house. Natalie pushed Porsha back and grabbed a
hold of Porsha's hair and threw her to the ground.

"Bitch you want to come to my home and cause trouble. Well, I
am going to give you some shit to think about the next time you want
to come over here." Natalie growled low in her throat as she began to
throw a couple of punches hitting Porsha in the mouth. She started
kicking Porsha in her face and tried to kick her in the stomach, but
Porsha blocked the kicks to her stomach with her hands. Jason and
Mrs. Lee ran outside. Jason swooped Natalie up in his arms while
Mrs. Lee helped Porsha up from the ground.

"Jason you better keep your bitch from coming to my home if you
know what's good for the both of you." Natalie pants as she jerked
away from him and walked into the house, slamming the door behind
her.

"Jason, you need to handle this now!" Mrs. Lee told him as she
entered the house.

"Porsha, I don't know why you showed up at my home, but this
will not happen again. Do you understand?" Jason was now looking
Porsha evenly in her eyes.

"I only came to see if you want to go to the doctors with me since
I'm carrying your child," she said as she brushed the dirt off of her
pants.

"Porsha, you know damn well that I don't want to go to the doctor
with you. I'm not sure this is even my baby. For all I know, it could
be Rico's. How much is it going to cost you to get an abortion?"

"What! Are you out of your mind?"

"No, I want no parts of this child."

"Okay, well you don't have to be a part of this child's life and I'll never come here anymore… but know this, your child will be brought into this world, with or without your support."

Parked down the street, keeping his distance, he sat and watched the brawl between Porsha and Natalie. He wished he could be with Natalie and love her the way she should be loved. He knew Jason didn't deserve such a loving and caring person, but he knew his day was coming. He just had to be patient and wait.

Chapter Thirty-One

The Test-Eight months later

Natalie and Jason's marriage had been put to the test, but as people would have guessed, the marriage survived the worst--- adultery.

Natalie was out in the back in the pool while Jason and Lee sat alongside the pool playing cards.

"How about that," Jason said as he threw two cards down.

"Well, let's see if you can take that to the bank." Lee returned as she slammed down three Aces.

"Oh, you sly devil," Jason chuckled as he folded.

"Okay, that does it for me, I'm starving," Jason yelled over to Natalie as she finished her fifth lap in the pool. "What about you babe, you want something to eat?"

"I thought you would never ask," Natalie told him as she got out of the pool dripping wet while Jason eyed her like a piece of chocolate cake.

"Why are you looking at me like that?"

He pulled her to him. "If mom wasn't out here I would eat you up like a piece of cake."

"Oh really, well, we can go upstairs for a little bit if you want to."

"Let's go." Jason grinned as he allowed Natalie to enter the house before him.

Upstairs in the bedroom, Natalie took a shower to rinse off the chlorine from her body. Just as she finished, Jason stepped in the shower and backed her up against the wall. He kissed her on her neck as his finger search through the wilderness for her treasure. Jason fingers find the jackpot and went to work. He inserted two fingers inside her and began to move them in and out as his mouth teased her nipples. Natalie grabbed a hold of Jason's penis and moved her hand up and down as it got harder and longer. Natalie bent down and ran the tip of her tongue alongside his shaft before taking it into her mouth.

"Aw shit!" Jason said as Natalie's mouth went to work. "Baby I'm about to come."

Natalie looked up at Jason. "Let's take this to the bed."

Jason followed Natalie to the bedroom where she took control. She pushed Jason down on the bed and finished where she left off. Natalie inserted the dick back into her mouth and went in for the kill. Minutes later, she climbed on top of him and rode him for dear life until they both come.

"Damn baby that was good." Jason sighed.

Jason dosed off while Natalie was downstairs preparing dinner to bring upstairs for the two when Jason's cell phone went off. Natalie made her way upstairs and heard Jason on the phone talking to someone.

"Dammit Porsha, I told you I wanted nothing to do with a baby that's probably not even mine!"

Natalie entered the room carrying the tray and from the look on Jason's face, she could tell that it was trouble. Natalie put the tray down and looked over at Jason, who was now off the phone. "What's going on?"

Jason looked at Natalie. He was afraid to tell her remembering what she said she would do if Porsha had the baby.

"That was Porsha."

"I can tell that much. What does that bitch want?"

Scared of what might happen because life for him and Natalie had been great, Jason paused for a minute. "She had the baby."

"She what! What did I tell you I would do if she had that bastard?"

"Natalie, please, I had no control over that. I tried to pay her to get an abortion, but she wouldn't. I don't even believe the baby is mine."

Natalie knocked the tray of food over and stormed into the bathroom. She stood there looking at herself in the mirror. "How can I let this mother-fucker get away with this?" She asked herself. Natalie moved to the edge of the tub, sat down and cried. How can this woman give him something that she had not been able to do? How can she compete with Porsha and this baby?

Natalie was letting her pride get in the way of her decision.

After cleaning up the mess that Natalie made, Jason walked to the bathroom door. He stood there before knocking. "Natalie, sweetheart… we need to talk. We can't end something that has turned out so wonderful. Think about what you're doing."

"No mother-fucker, you should have thought about what you were doing before you fucked that bitch!" Natalie shouted as she swung the bathroom door open.

"Yeah, you're right. I should have thought with the head on my shoulders and not my other head. I take full responsibility for this, but please wait before you file for a divorce. What if this baby is not mine?"

"Well, you better hope that it's not yours. But in the meantime, I'm moving out."

"You're moving out." Jason was shaking his head. "Where are you going?"

"That's none of your damn business."
Natalie pulled a suitcase out of the closet and started to pack. Jason stood there, watching her pack her belongings. "Natalie, I wish you wouldn't do this right now. What can I do to make you stay?"

"I told you to make sure that baby wasn't born."

"Natalie, be for real. You know I had no control over that. Stop being ridiculous."

"Ridiculous… I am being ridiculous because my husband impregnated someone else. You are so full of shit Jason."

"If you leave, please let Lee know where you're going."
Natalie grabbed her purse and suitcase and headed downstairs. She walked into the kitchen looking for Lee.

"Hey Mrs. Lee, just so you know, I'm checking into the Embassy Suites hotel downtown until your son finds out if Porsha's baby is his or not."

"What?"

"Yeah, she called to tell him that she gave birth to the baby."

"Is it a boy or girl?"
Natalie looked at Mrs. Lee as if to say 'are you kidding'. Mrs. Lee hugged Natalie. "I wish you wouldn't leave, but if you must go, just be careful and phone me once you check into your hotel room."

"Okay."

Chapter Thirty-Two

The Break Up

Natalie checked into the hotel and phoned Lee as she promised she would do. After speaking with Lee, Natalie lay across the bed and thought about her life, her marriage and the unspeakable--- the baby. How could she stay married to a man that had a child with his mistress? Every time she sees the baby she would be reminded that her husband had an affair. There was no way on earth that she could ever get over this. The only way she saw her marriage surviving is if the baby was not Jason's. She knew that if they found out the baby was not Jason's, it will take some time to get their marriage back to where it was… if it ever could.

Two weeks later, Jason and Porsha sat in the doctor's office waiting to hear the results of the paternity test. Jason was on pins and needles. He wanted this over so he can get back with his wife. He missed her like crazy. He hadn't been able to talk with her since she left. She refused to take any of his calls. He knew she was okay because she and Lee spoke on a daily basis, but she had made it clear that she wanted nothing to do with him until she knew he was not the baby's father.
The doctor pulled out his files and sat behind his desk as he looked over the result.
"Well, are you guys ready?"
"Hell yeah!" Jason said.
"Okay, the test shows that Jason Jerome Jackson is 99.9 % not the baby's biological father."
Jason turned his burning gaze at Porsha. "I told you, you lying witch. You caused my wife to leave me behind your lies."
Jason turned back to the doctor. "I need a copy of that report so I can prove once and for all that I am not her baby's daddy," Jerome said as he paced back and forth in the doctor's office.
"Sure, let me have my assistant make you a copy."

Porsha sat in disbelief. She was so sure that Jason was the father, but now she knows it is Rico. Too bad her child will never see her father.

"I am so sorry, Jason. I swear I thought you were the father or at least I was hoping and praying you were." She said as she got up and walked to stand in front of Jason.

"Woman, do you know how much damage you have caused my marriage?" I never want to see or hear from you as long as I live. Do you understand that?"

The doctor's assistant walked in the room and handed Jason the result.

"Thank you," He said in a gruff voice before heading out.

Jason rushed to his car to phone Natalie. He could only hope she would take his call this time.

"Hello, Jason."

Hello, Natalie. I have some good news. Like I tried to tell you, the baby is not mine." There was a sigh on her end of the connection.

"I'm glad to hear that Jason, but that doesn't change the fact that you cheated on me. I thought I was over this, but I guess I'm not. I need some time to work through this, so I've decided to get my own place until I can face the fact that the man I loved with all my heart, cheated on me."

Jason sat stunned. He thought telling her the news would have her running back to him, but her response had put him in an awkward place.

"Are you sure this is what you want to do?"

"No, I am not sure, but I know this is what needs to be done.

"Natalie, I wish you wouldn't do this. I wish you would come home. I'll give you your space."

"Jason no, I don't think you understand how this has affected me and until you do, we will never be good together."

"So what are you saying, Natalie? Are you telling me that you want a divorce?"

"No, that's not what I am saying, but if I can't get over this, then that's what will happen."

It had been two weeks and still no word from Natalie. Jason felt as though his marriage was over. Natalie moved into her apartment and each day Lee heard less and less from Natalie. She refused to tell Lee where she had moved fearing that Lee would tell Jason. This didn't seem like the same person Jason was married to for six and a half years.

Jason tried to go on with his life and his new career, but it was hard. He continued to beat himself up for ever getting involved with Porsha again.

Jason was busy at his desk looking over a case James brought to his attention yesterday when there was a knock on the door. Jason looked up. "Come on in."

James came in. "Have you had time to look over the case?"

"I'm doing that right now."

"Have you heard from Natalie?" James asked.

"No, I was just thinking about her. I think I really fucked up this time. I can't sleep at night. I can't focus when I am here; I don't know what I'm going to do."

"You are going to make it, that's what you're going to do. In time, Natalie will come around and see that she needs and wants you in her life, but it will take some time. In the meantime, I suggest you do nothing to screw this up this time."

Chapter Thirty-Three

Mending a Broken Heart

Natalie tried her best to get on with her life, but it wasn't easy. Her heart felt as if it had been broken into pieces. She wanted so badly to cheat on Jason--- to let him know how it felt--- but the opportunity hadn't presented itself, as of yet. Natalie had even caught herself trying to draw certain male attention in order to start a fling with him, then somehow let Jason find out about it. Natalie was busy trying to come up with a plan when she thought she saw a familiar face.

"It can't be," she thought to herself.

Natalie was having lunch in one of the restaurants downtown. She didn't realize that she had been followed for the last month. This person knew her every move. He knew what time she normally went to bed, what time she woke up and left for work; he even knew the time she took her lunch break. This person was in love with Natalie and would stop at nothing to have her.

Natalie got up to leave when she thought she saw this person again. She couldn't get a good look at this person, but something about him was familiar to her. Natalie tried to catch up with this person, but by the time she made it outside, he was gone. Walking to her car she got an uneasy feeling that she was being watched. Natalie made it back to work with five minutes to spare. She pulled into the parking garage, cuts the engine and grabbed her purse. She headed for the elevator in the parking garage when she heard footsteps behind her. When she turned, there was no one there, so she continued to walk and again she heard footsteps, but this time, she continued walking without looking behind her and took the stairs instead of waiting for the elevator.

Driving home from work, Natalie was tired of not being able to sleep at night. Her mind continued to stay on her husband and what he was or was not doing. She wondered, since her departure, had he been in contact with Porsha. She was cognizant that in the beginning of their marriage, there was someone who had hurt Jason bad and now she knew it was Porsha. What she couldn't understand is why anyone in their right mind would risk losing their wife over someone who broke their heart. Maybe he wasn't really over her.

Natalie pulled into her reserve parking space, unaware of her surroundings. She cuts the engine, grabbed her purse, briefcase, and exited the car. She took her time walking up the walkway enjoying the warm summer breeze and the sound of laughter coming from the children down the street.

As she entered the townhouse, the feeling of loneliness hit her like a ton of bricks. "I can't go on like this," she whispered to herself. Natalie moved further into the living room, discarding her purse and briefcase. Natalie began to pace back and forth debating on whether she should call Jason and tell him she wanted him and needed him right now. She continued to fight with her pride. Her pride would not allow her to make the phone call to her husband, so she went upstairs to her bedroom, removed her clothing and hopped in the shower. As she stood in the stall, the warm water ran down her body relaxing every inch of her stressed body until thoughts of Jason and Porsha together clouded her mind, making her angry all over again. For some reason, she simply could not let it go that Jason cheated on her. She began to wonder what Porsha did sexually to Jason that had him still interested in her after almost seven years.

After dinner, Natalie relaxed out front on her porch with a romance novel called, 'Careless Whisper'. The more she read, the more she wanted her husband. "I wish someone would make me feel like I'm everything to them." She mumbled to herself as she continued to read the novel by Rochelle Alers.

Later that night, Natalie lay awake in bed… another sleepless night. She glanced at the nightstand. The alarm clock reads 2:30 am.

"Damn, I need some sleep."

Out of nowhere, Natalie's hand grabbed a hold of the phone on the nightstand. Before she knew it, she had dialed Jason's number.

"What if he has someone there with him? What if he doesn't want me back?" All of these things ran through her mind as she waited for him to answer. On the fifth ring, Natalie hung up. She felt deflated and hurt that he didn't answer.

Jason had stepped out of the shower when he heard his phone ring. He rushed to answer, but by the time he got there, the caller had hung up. He checked the number and realized it was Natalie. His heart was beating rapidly while dialing her number. He only hoped she was okay.

"Hello?"

"Natalie, is everything okay?"

"Yes… I mean no, Jason. Everything is not okay." Natalie decided to put her pride aside. "I need you, Jason. I need you now."

Jason wiped the perspiration from his forehead. "Oh is that so? And how bad do you need me?"

"Why don't you come over here and find out."

"I would, but you know there's just one little problem."

Natalie's heart dropped to her stomach. She didn't want to hear what she thought he was going to say.

"I don't know where you live."

Natalie laughed out loud. "Oh my God, I thought you were going to tell me that you didn't want to see me."

"Natalie sweetheart, you should know better than that. I know I've not been the perfect husband, but I love you more than life and if I'm given a second chance, I'll make you see this each and every day as long as I live. Now give me the address." They both laughed.

Jason drove through red lights going seventy mph on the interstate, weaving in and out of the few cars out on the road. He hoped he didn't get pulled over, but he couldn't wait to see Natalie and wrap his arms around her and show her how much he loved her and how much he was so in love with her. He wanted her to know that his life was incomplete without her.

Natalie was busy in the bathroom freshening up for her husband when she sees a shadow move in her bedroom. She stood in shock too frightened to move. She slowly looked around the bathroom for something she can use as a weapon when she sees her curling irons. She quickly plugged them into the wall. Natalie refused to move. If she was going to be attacked, it will be in the light where she can see and fight back using her curling irons.

Just as she was about to unplug the irons a figure appeared in the doorway. Natalie screamed as she backed further into the bathroom.

"Who the fuck are you?" Natalie screamed.

The intruder didn't answer. The person just stood there, looking Natalie up and down.

"You're a pretty little bitch," The intruder said, trying to disguise their voice.

"What? Do I know you?"

Natalie's eyes almost popped out of their sockets when the intruder raised their hand. In it was a knife that looked sharp enough to slice through a walnut like warm butter.

"Please, don't hurt me," Natalie begged. "Take whatever you want. I have money in my wallet."

"Bitch, I don't want your money. I want you buried six feet under," the intruder said.

The intruder began to stab Natalie continuously and with no mercy. When the intruder stopped, blood was everywhere. On the walls, the mirror, the towels hanging in the bathroom--- and the intruder. The intruder was completely drenched in Natalie's blood.

This person staggered back, dropping the knife and turned to run out of Natalie's Townhome.

Jason pulled up just in time to see someone dressed in all black running down the walkway. He double-checked the address and realized this was Natalie's place this person just ran from.

Jason hopped out of his vehicle, leaving the car door wide open with the keys still in the ignition and ran towards the front door where he sees blood. He panicked as he ran in yelling for Natalie.

"Nat, are you okay? Where are you, Natalie?" He yelled as he ran upstairs to the bedroom where he sees Natalie lying in a pool of blood on the bathroom floor.

"Natalie, Natalie!" Jason screamed as he ran to her and pulled her into his lap.

"Oh baby baby baby baby no no no-no," he cried out. Who would do this to you? Jason asked her softly, cradling her.

Jason nervously pulled out his phone and dialed 911.

Jason, James, John, and Lee wait patiently in the waiting room at the hospital. Jason phoned Natalie's parent and explained to them what had happened and advised them to get there ASAP because he feared the worst. He feared Natalie would not pull through after seeing all the blood and to learn that she has been stabbed seventeen times. He also learned that one of her lungs had collapsed. Jason could not imagine why or who would want to harm her...

Chapter Thirty-Four

The Unexpected

The old couple walked as fast as their legs could possibly go.

"I knew I should have reached out to my baby, but no, you continued to forbid me to talk with her. Now my baby is fighting for her life. I have missed her so much," Natalie's mother Mrs. Robinson bit out.

"I'm sorry, sweetheart. I'm sorry I kept you from our daughter. I was being stubborn, I would never have guessed things would have turned out like this."

"Her being married to that low down drug dealer, what would one expect. I just hope now her eyes are opened to the danger he has caused her and divorce him."

"Not now Meredith, we don't even know the circumstances. Let's just hear what he has to say before we jump to any conclusion."

"I guess you're right Frank."

Frank and Meredith approached Jason as he lay asleep in his chair next to Lee.

Meredith bent down and touched Jason on the leg. "Jason is that you?"

Jason awoke to the surprise of his life. He did not believe that Natalie's parents would actually show up, he had only hoped they would.

"Yes, it's me. I am so glad you guys made it here to see Natalie." Jason stood to his feet. "Can we talk?" Jason asked.

"Yes, we need to know what happened to our baby," Meredith said as the tears began to roll down her face.

Jason guided the couple in the sitting area in the corner of the waiting room. He began to explain from the very beginning when everyone thought he was a thug and a drug dealer.

It was Natalie's father that spoke first. "Oh my God Jason, we had no idea. I am so embarrassed. A man of God and I treated you and my only child the way I did. I hope you can find it in your heart to forgive us."

"All is forgiven. The most important thing is that you're here now and that Natalie pulls through to restore the relationship that she had with her parents before I came into the picture."

Meredith reached over and embraced Jason. "I'm so glad Natalie had someone like you in her life who loves her so much."

Jason placed his hands on his face as he reared back in the chair. He blamed himself for this. If he hadn't been so weak when it came to Porsha, none of this would have happened. He would have been home in bed with his wife.

Natalie had been in surgery for over five hours. The doctors were working hard to stop the internal bleeding. An hour later, Natalie's doctor emerged from surgery and into the waiting area.

He walked over to the nurse's station. "I need to speak to the Jackson family."

The nurse walked over to Jason. "Mr. Jackson, the doctor will speak with you now."

The whole family jumped from their seat and followed the nurse to the doctor who was waiting in the hallway.

"Hello, I'm Doctor Stevens. I'm Natalie's doctor." The doctor looked at how many family members and friends were present. "If you guys don't mind, we can sit and talk at the other end of the waiting area."

As the family sat, their hearts were beating so fast that Jason thought his heart would jump out of his chest at any minute. "Doctor, please, tell us what Natalie's condition is."

"As you know she lost a lot of blood from the seventeen stab wounds. It took almost four hours just to get the bleeding stopped, but we were able to get that under control. One of her lungs had collapsed, but other than that, I think she'll pull through. I will keep her in Intensive Care overnight just to see how she does. She cannot have any visitors at this time and before I forget, the police will be here tomorrow to speak with you, Jason."

"I've already spoken with them and told them everything I know. I know right now that I am a suspect and I can handle that, but I will not continue to waste my time talking to the police. I will find this person myself and when I do, they will wish the police had found them first and locked them up---. You can believe that."

"You can count us in on the search." James and John chimed in.

Jason looked over at the Robinson's. "I almost forgot. Mr. & Mrs. Robinson, this is my mom Lee Jackson."

"How do you do," Mr. Robinson said politely.

"You must think we're terrible parents," Mrs. Robinson said softly.

"Under the circumstances, I understand." Lee smiled gently.

"Mom, I'm going to spend the night here. Why don't you and the Robinson's go home? Jason turned to the couple. "Natalie and I have plenty of room for you to stay with us for as long as you like."

"Oh, how sweet of you, Jason," Mrs. Robinson said with a sincere heart.

The family continued to linger around the hospital for another hour before heading home. Lee set the Robinson's up in one of the guest rooms. Jason had spoken to James and John earlier and asked if they would both stay at the house with Lee as well.

"You know my heart is so heavy right now. I feel so bad for the way we treated Jason and our baby and look what happened to her. How can I ever forgive myself?" Mrs. Robinson was crying.

"I know, I'm ashamed, too. We'll have to do whatever it takes to make it up to them. I just pray our baby pulls through." Mr. Robinson walked over to his wife and kneeled down to pray. Mrs. Robinson joined her husband on her knees and began to pray with him.

Downstairs, Lee sat at the kitchen table staring into space. She couldn't believe the events that had transpired this year.

Lord, things have got to get better." She said out loud.

"They will trust me," James responded as he walked in.

Lee looked up. "How long have you been standing there?"

"Not long. Just long enough to know that you need to be resting."

"I couldn't rest if I wanted to."

Lee stood and walked over to the sink where she broke down.

"Who would do this to her," she cried as James walked over to comfort her. The feel of the strong man's arms around her made her even weaker, especially since it was James. The smell of his cologne turned her on. The way he was looking at her made her want to jump right into bed with him. The more she was around James, the deeper she was falling in love with him.

His body felt so good that she didn't want to let him go. His dark gray eyes burned a hole right through her soul and his complexion looked like it was glistening. The eyes, the skin, and feel of his hard body against hers and the smell of his cologne was enough to drive her wild

Chapter Thirty-Five

Getting your feelings under control

James was ten years older than Jason and John and ten years younger than Lee. James had developed feelings for Lee while at the cabin and the condo, but he down- played his feelings because of Jason, but now he wanted to know if Lee still felt for him what he was feeling for her. The two hadn't been together since the night at the celebration,but when they did see each other, it was hard for them to be in the same room.

As the two embrace each other, he felt his heart skip a beat. He had never felt this way about anyone in his life and it scared him.

James took a step back and placed his hands on Lee's shoulder.

"Lee things will get better trust me," He told her as he looked at her, searching for any traces of regret and when he didn't find any he pulled her close to him. He placed his hand on the back of her head as she closed her eyes lying against his chest.

"Lee, what are we doing?" You know how Jason is going to feel if he finds out about us."

"Enjoying each other's company, is something wrong with that?"

"No, not at all, but you know what we are up against."

"Why do you worry about Jason? The way I see it, we are both grown as hell and what I chose to do and who I chose to do it with is not any of Jason's business."

James laughed, "You are one feisty woman."

Lee looked up at James. She didn't know when she developed feeling for him, but right now if she wasn't careful, they just might end up in bed together.

"You know I love Jason like a younger brother and I would hate to lose him as a friend, but Lee I feel if two people care about each other no one should stand in their way of happiness."

"Here here, I do agree. So what are we going to do about these feelings?"

"I say we take things a little slow and let's not tell Jason just yet. The last thing I want to do is hurt one of my best friend's."

"Deal," Lee stepped in. "But before we start taking it slow, I want you to kiss me."
James laughed as he pulled Lee to him. "You are something else."
James looked down at her and planted little kisses on her forehead.
He moved down to her nose and then brushed his lips across her lips.
Lee opened her mouth to let him in. James took it slow at first, but the feelings that went through his body would not allow him to take his time.
James kissed Lee with so much desire, and she was right there with him. The fire between the two was so hot that if they were not careful someone could possibly get burned.
John stood in the entryway of the door, furious. He could not believe what he was witnessing. John made a noise which caused the two to separate.

"What the hell is going on, James?"

"What does it look like, John. Two grown- ass people kissing."

"I can't believe you. You're taking advantage of Lee."
Lee spoke up. "Now wait a minute, John. Nobody is taking advantage of anyone. I happen to be attracted to James and I have been for some time now. I'm sorry that we decided to do something about how we feel about each other now, but sometimes you just can't control your feeling… you have to let them loose at some point."
It was James' turn. "John, I know you care deeply for Lee, but I care about her as well just in a different way. Why can't I be happy with whomever I want? You know I am a damn good guy and so does Jason."
John shook his head at the two as he walked out of the kitchen down the hall to his room.

"Lee, I think we need to sit down and talk. I don't want to cause a rift between Jason and us."
James and Lee walked outside to the back on the deck. James took a seat while Lee stood.

"James, I have never felt more alive than I do right now.
You've stirred something up inside of me and I love the feeling.
Please don't let my son or John stand in the way of us finding out if we're good together. Please, I beg you."
James walked over and stood by her. "Lee, what I feel right now for you is real, very real and I will not let anyone stand in the way of us

being together if that's what we both want. However, I don't want to cause any problems for you and Jason. This's my biggest issue."
Lee looked at him. "You know when we were on our way to the condo and you touched my face to talk to me about Jason? I wanted you so badly, but I didn't know how you would feel if I had said something."
Lee rubbed her hand across James' face. In turn, he kissed her hand.

"Women, I don't know what I'm going to do about you. You make it hard for me to take it slow with you. If I didn't know any better, I would think you're doing this on purpose."

"Doing what on purpose?"

"Turning me on."
Just as James said this Lee felt a tingling below. "Oh, James, you don't know what you're doing to me right now. I think we better call it a night before I do something outrageous."
James moved closer to Lee and wrapped his arms around her waist.

"How outrageous?"

"Let me just show you."
Lee stuck her tongue gently in James' ear as she rubbed his dick until it became long and hard.

"Oh, Lee... please stop. You don't know what you are starting."

"Don't worry, because whatever I start I can damn sure finish it."
Lee unfastened James pants and pulled his dick out.

"Damn James, I almost forgot what you were working with. Let me show you how good I can make you feel."

"Lee, please stop," James groaned as Lee ran her tongue around his head. She licked James's dick from side to side.

"Damn this shit feels so good." Lee slowly took him in and deep throats him.

"Lee you better stop, baby, I'm about to come."
Lee removed James' long cock from her mouth and guided him to one of the chairs on the deck. She pushed him down as she straddled him and inserted his big dick inside of her and started twerking that ass on him, driving James crazy.

"Damn, Lee, you're going to make me marry that ass."
Minutes later, the two lay in each other's arms fast asleep.

Chapter Thirty-Six

Moving Too Fast

Early that morning, John stood looking out on the deck watching Lee and James lay together while sleeping. He went back into his room and brought out a blanket and laid it across the two. He knew it would only be a short time before Jason learned about his mother and one of his best friends, relationship and then all hell would break loose. "I just hope they know what they are doing," Johns sighed as he moved to the kitchen to make breakfast for everyone.

Lee awoke first and woke James, "Oh my God, I hope Jason hasn't made it home yet."

Lee made her way inside and goes to the kitchen where she sees John making breakfast. The look on her face said it all.

"Don't worry your secret is still safe. Jason hasn't made it home yet."

"What secret?" Jason asked as he made his way into the kitchen. Lee attempted to play it off and change the subject. "Has there been any improvement in Natalie's condition?"

"No, not yet. The doctor wants to keep her in ICU another night. Have her parents been down?"

"Not yet," John replied.

"So what's this secret you guys were talking about when I came in?"

Just then James walked in. "I'm staying out of it. This will be between you and Lee." John said, going back to the cooking.

"Mom, what's going on?"

"I have a love interest that John found out about."

James almost shits on himself when he heard Lee say this.

"Well, that's nice. Who is he?"

"That's for me to know and you to find out when I feel the time is right."

"That's cool, just as long as he treats you right. If not, he'll have to deal with us."

James and John exchanged a glance. "That's right, he'd better treat her right," John remarked as James rolled his eyes at him.

"Mom, why don't you go up and freshen up and then tell the Robinson's to come on down for breakfast."

Jason waited for Lee to leave the kitchen before walking over to John. "Who was here with my mom last night?"

"No one… why?"

"Because she smells of sex."

John glanced at James. "James, was there anyone here with Lee last night?"

"And how would I know that?"

"You two were the last ones in the kitchen last night."

"I think you need to ask her who she was with last night. I'm not her babysitter." With that, James walked out of the kitchen to the room he was supposed to be sleeping in.

"What's eating him?" Jason asked.

"Guilt."

"Guilt, what do you mean guilt?"

"I am staying out of it so you should talk to him about what's eating at him."

Fifteen minutes later, everyone was gathered in the kitchen eating breakfast before heading out to the hospital. Lee was in the best mood that Jason had seen her in years. He chalked it up to her love interest. Jason was happy for his mom in a big way. He knew she deserved to be happy and have someone love her the way he loved his wife. He knew it wouldn't be easy, knowing that his mom was dating someone. For so many years Lee had devoted her time to him and when Nat came along, she devoted her time to the both of them. Losing Lee to another man would not be easy, but he would do his best to handle it in a good way.

"Mom, I want you and the Robinson to ride with John to the hospital because I'm staying the night with Nat again."

"If you don't mind, I will ride with James."

"Sure, whatever."

Lee placed her hand on James' thigh under the table. James smiled and placed his hand on top of hers. He felt a little silly acting like a schoolboy with his first crush.

At the hospital, Natalie was still unable to have any visitors, yet, but the doctor was hopeful that she will recover well. He just wanted to make sure that the bleeding had stopped.

John sat in the corner, continuing to eye James and Lee, who was acting like teenagers in love. Jason was too busy talking to the doctor trying to ease his way into see Natalie to pay any attention to them. Jason sweet- talked one of the nurses into letting him in to see Natalie just for a quick second.

John couldn't take it anymore and approached the two. "Why don't you guys act your age and give Jason a little more respect than what you're giving him. You both know it's going to be hard for him to handle this when he finds out about you two. Let him find out when Natalie's better."

"I hate to say it, but he's right." James nodded as he rolled his eyes at John. "I think we need to cool it for a while."

Lee felt like she just got hit with a daggered. She got up and made her way to the ladies room. In no way does she want James to see her cry. Lee hadn't been this happy in years, and now, she has to go back being alone and lonely. Lee stayed in the ladies room a little too long for James. He made his way to the door and knocked before calling out to her. "Lee, are you okay?" But there was no answer. James knocked again before entering. There he found Lee standing at the sink in tears.

"Lee, what's the matter?"

"I am so tired of watching people around me be happy and in love and the one chance that I have at being happy, I can't. This is not fair, James. I want to be happy and be in love with someone."

"I know Lee, I feel the same way, but we need to give Jason some time and then we can approach him about us. I have never felt this way about anyone and I will be damned if I let you get away from me just like that. I will fight for us and I hope you will be right there fighting beside me."

James and Lee got caught by a nurse in the ladies restroom kissing.

"Excuse me, sir, but you're in the ladies restroom."

James and Lee burst out laughing.

"I'm sorry, I'm leaving now."

Lee waited a few minutes before leaving the ladies room. As she headed out the door, she bumped into John, who was coming out of

the men's restroom and noticed that Lee had been crying. "Lee I hope I didn't upset you earlier by what I said to you and James."
She looked at him with reddened eyes. "John, have you ever been in love, or liked someone so much that you thought you would lose your mind?"

"I'm afraid I have."

"Then you know what I'm feeling right now and to have you tell me that James and I need to cool it crushed me. John, I have never felt this way since I was with my late husband and you know how long he's been dead. I'm not getting any younger, and my days are numbered so why can't I be happy while I'm here on this earth?"
Lee left John standing and thinking about what she said. He knew exactly how she felt.

Chapter Thirty-Seven

The Recovery Process

Two weeks later, Natalie was doing much better. Today was the day that she could finally come home and live in her home with her husband. She was thrilled when she opened her eyes two weeks ago and sees her parents for the first time in almost seven years. The tears that she held back all these years flowed uncontrollably for her parents. It was a little too much for Jason to bear so he left them alone in her room to get reunited with each other.

James and Lee had been secretly meeting with each other every day. The more they saw each other, the more they fell in love. They were at the point in their life where they wanted to move in with each other. The time was coming soon for them to have that talk with Jason about their relationship, but each day they continued to put it off for fear of it causing problems, problems that they do not need.

Lee was in Natalie's room sitting on the side of the bed with her when she asked, "Ms. Lee, can I ask you a question?"

Lee smiled a little. "Okay, now that you know I am not the housekeeper, you need to drop the Ms. and just call me Lee."

Natalie laughed, "Okay... Lee. Why are you so happy nowadays? I know Jason said you were seeing someone, but we've never met him and I never hear you talk about him."

"Oh, Nat, it's complicated. I love this man so much and unfortunately, we have to keep each other a secret from my son."

"But why, Jason wants to see you happy and in love with someone."

"That might be true, but he might not agree with whom I'm seeing or in love with."

Natalie looked at Lee strange.

"Now I'm afraid to ask who he is."

"Then don't. If you don't know then Jason can't be mad at you when he finds out. Natalie, I really want to move in with this person."

"Is it that serious?"

"Yes, it is. Enough about me, how are you doing?"

"I'm doing better each day, but I'm getting tired of the detectives coming around asking me question after question.
I just want to forget about it and move on."

"Well, they aren't going to rest until that person is caught and besides that... Jason, John and James will not rest either."
Natalie noticed how Lee's eyes lit up whenever she mentioned James' name.

"Is there something I should know about you and James?"
Lee stared at Natalie before she let the biggest smile show.

"I don't know, why you would ask me that being that he is one of my son's best friends!" Lee exclaimed as she gave Natalie a look that said you hit the nail on the head. Just then, there was a knock at the door.

"Come in," Natalie called out.

"Oh! My two favorite girls," Jason grinned as he entered the bedroom.

"What are you girls up to?"

"Oh, just having a little girl talk." Natalie smiled at Lee.

"When do we get to meet the mystery- man, Mom?"

"In due time," Lee returned primly as she got up off of the bed.

"I'll leave you two alone. I'll be in my room if you need anything, Nat."

"I got her, Mom. You and Mrs. Robinson can relax today. Why don't you guys go shopping or something?"

"That sounds good, but I already made plans today." She winked at Natalie.

"Well, maybe we can have a cookout today," Jason nodded as he looked at Natalie. "Are you up for it? All you have to do is sit there and look pretty... we'll do everything else."

"That sounds good to me, but right now I need a nap."

Lee was busy getting dressed for her date when she heard a knock at her door. "Come in."
James walked in looking sexier than ever and smelling so good that he instantly turned her on. He shut the door, locked it and moved further into the room until he was standing in front of Lee. James bent down and kissed her on the lips. "Hello, precious."

"Hey, sweetie. You know you're taking a chance of Jason catching us."

"Right now, I don't care. I want you and I don't care who knows it anymore."

"Well James, I do. I don't want to ruin your friendship with Jason or my relationship with my son. So we'll have to be careful until the time is right, but I think Natalie knows."

"Do you think she'll tell Jason?"

"No, not at all."

"How about we stop off at my place before we head downtown if that's okay."

"Sure, that's fine. Now go and I'll meet you at our secret location."

"Okay," James said softly as he kissed her before he left.
Jason was down the hall from Lee's room when he sees James leaving out of her room. Jason thought nothing of it and went on about his business.

When Lee arrived at the secret location she sees James had already made it there. He was so punctual. Lee parked, got out of her car and walked over to James's car. James got out and walked around to the passenger's side and opened the door for Lee.

"Thank you. You are such a gentlemen."

"I will always be gentlemen when it comes to you," James grinned as he closed Lee's door.
Lee looked over at James as he maneuvered his car into traffic. She loved everything about this man from the top of his wavy hair down to his muscular bowlegs.

"Why don't you take a picture, it will last longer," James said as he noticed how Lee was checking him out.

"You're such a smart- ass."

"Yeah, and that's why you love me."

"Who says I love you?"

"Oh, you tell me that everything we make love."
Lee grinned. Just mentioning the words, making love had her insides on fire.
Lee looked over at James. "James, will our relationship always be like this? I feel so good whenever I'm with you or just thinking about you."

"Why wouldn't it be? A relationship or marriage is all about what you make of it. If you want it to be good, then you work hard at making it good. That's what some people don't understand."

James pulled into his driveway, cut the engine and took his keys out of the ignition. He looked at Lee and started to laugh.

"What's funny?"

"You," James said as he exited the car and made his way around to her side.

"What did I do or say?"

"You didn't do or say anything. You have no idea how much I love you, do you?"

Chapter Thirty-Eight

Too Much For Her to Handle

"Stay here I have a surprise for you," James smiled at Lee.
He went back to his bedroom and got the Tiffany box off of his
dresser. He opened it up to get a look at it before he gave it to Lee. He
hoped she liked it as much as he did.

"This is for you. I bought this earlier when I was out shopping. I
saw this and knew I wanted you to have it."

"What is it?"

"Why don't you open it up and find out."
Lee's eyes widened with delight. "Oh my God, I love it. It's my
birthstone!"
James slid the ring on her finger on her right hand. She held the ring
up to get a better look at it.

"James, what will I tell people when they ask me about the ring?"

"You can tell them whatever you want to tell them. I told you I'm
tired of hiding our relationship."
With that, he simply wrapped his arms around her and started
planting little kisses to her neck.

"James, what are you up to? I thought we were going downtown
and walk around a little bit."

"We can still do that after I get me some."
Lee turned to face James and looked him in the eyes. "You are
something else… you know that."

"I'm getting ready to be a satisfied man in a little bit."
James guided Lee down the hall to his bedroom. "Have you thought
about moving in with me?"

"You know I have and I want to, but right now isn't the time.'

"When will be the right time, Lee?"

"James, please give me more time," Lee whispered with tears in
her eyes.

"Sweetheart, don't cry. I'll give you all the time you need, but if
Jason asks me, about us, I won't lie. Now come here." James said as
he parted her lips with his tongue.

Lee opened up a little more, allowing James full access to her mouth.
James deepened the kiss and with his hands, he started to unbutton
her blouse. He reached behind her and unfastened her bra allowing
her breasts to rest freely. James began to rub her nipples until they
become hard as his tongue flicked across the nipple before taking it
into his mouth.

Lee reached for James's belt and unfastened it. She went for his pants
next unbuttoning and sliding the zipper down, pulling his big, thick
dick out for her to admire.

"Oh, I love this." She smiled as she moved her hand up and down
and across the head as the pre-cum seeped out. Lee got down on her
knees and took him in her mouth. James threw his head back and
enjoyed the feeling of her wet juicy lips wrapped around him.

"Oh baby, do big daddy good."

Before he came, James removed himself from Lee's mouth and
finished undressing her. When she was completely naked, he turned
her around and bent her over the bed and inserted himself inside of
her ass.

"Oh hell naw!" Lee yelled. The pain in her ass was unbearable.

"It's only going to hurt for a minute… I promise." James
continued to stroke her slowly trying to lessen the pain. He reached
around in front of Lee and unfolded her lips and gently started to rub
her womanly nub until Lee forgot about the pain.

"Oh, James, this feels so damn good."

"Oh baby, please come with me. Oh, shit this ass feels so damn
good.

"Oh Lee!" James cried out as he and Lee both exploded.

 Lee fell to the bed, bringing James down with her with his dick still
inside her ass.

A few hours later, Lee arrived home just in time for dinner.

Lee slowly made her way upstairs to her room. Her ass was killing
her. That would be the last time that I let James screw me in my ass,
she thought.

Lee changed into something more comfortable before heading out
back to the cookout. She was in a hurry to get out there to see James
that she forgot to take off her ring.

Lee stood in the doorway, scanning the back yard for James. John
walked up behind her. "He's not here yet."

Lee made her way out back and took a seat next to Mrs. Robinson.

"So how are you guys enjoying your stay here?"

"We love it, but we have to leave later on this evening. My husband has his job to get back to and seeing that Natalie is in such good hands, I feel better leaving her."

"I'm just glad you guys were able to work out your differences."

"Me too. This has opened my eyes to realize that life is too short to not speak or to be around your loved ones because you never know when God is going to call them home."

Lee looked up and sees James standing in the corner talking with Jason. The look on her face told it all. Anyone who knew her knew she was definitely in love and it was written all over her face, especially when James was around.

James and Jason joined the group at the table. Jason sat across from her while James took a seat right next to her.

"Where did you get that ring mom?"

"From someone special… why?" Lee asked as she held her hand out for Natalie to inspect. "It's pretty isn't it?"

John grinned. He had never seen Mrs. Lee like this. She acted like a schoolgirl and James didn't act any older. However, he knew all hell was about to break loose once Jason caught on to them.

"How are those ribs coming along?" Lee asked.

"I don't know let me check." John was still grinning.

"Don't move I'll get it," Lee said, getting up with a grimace. Lee slowly made her way over to the grill and everyone noticed how she was walking.

"Mom, are you okay?"

"Yes, I am fine, why?"

"You're walking a little funny, dear."

John looked at Natalie as she began to laugh. They could only imagine as to why Mrs. Lee was walking funny.

John looked at James and shook his head. "You're one sick bastard," he said as he got up from the table.

"Did I miss something, James?" Jason asked.

James threw up his hands as if he had no clue as to why John said what he just said.

"I think someone needs to let me in on the secret."

"Jason, you know just as much as I do." James winked.

Lee overheard the conversation at the table and knew that all hell was about to break loose if she didn't do something.

"Jason baby, can I talk to you for a minute."

"Sure, Mom, what's the problem?" Jason called back to her as he walked over to his mom.

"There's no problem, sweetie. I just want to tell you something." James got up from the table and made his way inside. He knew it was time for him to leave before Lee broke the news to Jason.

"Walk down here with me," Lee said, patting him on the arm.

"I want you to understand how the person that I am seeing makes me feel. I have never felt this good in my life ever, not even with your father. I want your permission to continue to feel this way and understand that people cannot help who they fall in love with."

"Okay... so what are you trying to tell me?

Chapter Thirty-Nine

When all hell breaks loose

"**Jason**, the man that I have been seeing and the man that I am in love with is someone that you're close to."

Jason nodded slowly, a bit mystified. "Someone I am close to. I am only close to John and Jam..." He stopped short, looking at his mother.

"Oh, don't tell me. Don't tell me that it's James because I will beat his ass." Jason turned and ran inside the house to look for James. "Jason you come back here!" Lee yelled as she tried to make her way in the house, hoping James had already left.

John grabbed a hold of Jason trying to keep him from leaving the house to go after James.

"See, this is the reason why I didn't want to tell you. I am a grown ass woman. I should be free to love and be with whomever I chose to, Jason."

"You can, just not one of my best friends. I am going to kill him... I promise you."

"Jason please calm down and don't you dare lay a hand on James."

"What, you're taking up for him now?"

"Yes, I am. I am sorry Jason but I love him. I am as much to blame as James is." Lee said as she began to cry. "I just want to be happy Jason and I'm sorry that I found happiness with one of your best friends."

Lee was so emotional that it made her sick to her stomach. She made her way up to her room where she broke down completely.

"Oh God, please help me. I don't want to lose the man I love because my son can't deal with the fact that I found love with his best friend."

Lee paced back and forth in her room. She was fighting with herself about what she needed to do. Lee knew that she might have to make a choice between Jason and James. She had always vowed that she would never allow a man to come between her and her son. It didn't matter that Jason was a grown man. She still valued his opinions and cared about his happiness and if her being with James interfered with his happiness then she will have to make things right.

The next day, Lee sat in her room trying to build up enough courage to call James. Lee finally picked up the phone. She quickly dialed his number before she had a chance to change her mind.
James answered on the third ring. "Hello beautiful, how are you and how are things this morning?"

"Oh, James, things are about the same. I've been in my room ever since you left yesterday. I've never seen Jason so upset. I'm so glad you decided to leave because I would've hated to see what would've happened if you stayed.

"I know. I know how much Jason cares about you and I know he wants nothing but the best, but he knows me so well. He knows I would never do anything to hurt you in any way."

"Jason knows this. It's just the fact that I'm his mom. If I was his sister, I guarantee you he wouldn't have a problem with this at all."

"Jason needs to know that we love each other. We have to make him see that I make you happy and you make me happy. Your happiness should be his concern and not that you're dating one of his best friends."
Lee sighed. "James, that's easier said than done."

"Why don't you come over here and we can sit and think of a way that will make Jason see what's important here."

"I think Jason needs to see the fact that without you in my life, how much I would hurt and how unhappy I would be, and the only way to do this is to..."

"Is to what?"

"Break this off until we can see each other without any problems."
There was a long pause. "Lee, don't do this baby. I need you in my life right now. I have never felt this way about anyone."

"James, I made a promise to myself when Jason's dad died that I would never allow a man to come between my son and me and to this day, I have kept that promise. As much as I hate to do this, I know right now it's the right thing to do. You need to remember I love you very much and I will do whatever it takes for us to be together and be happy... but you have to promise me that you won't allow any women in your life while I try to work things out with Jason."

She could tell James was angry now: furious, actually. "Lee, I won't promise you that. What if you can't convince Jason to accept that we want to be together? Where does that leave me?"
Lee felt as though her heart had just broken in half. "James please promise me you won't date anyone. I will do whatever it takes to make Jason see we belong together."
James' voice was stiff now. "Like I said before, I can't and won't promise you that." He was angry and hurt. He knew he had no intention of seeing anyone, but he didn't want Lee to know that. He knew getting involved with her would backfire on him because he knew how Jason felt when it came to his mom, but he figured because it was him, he knew Jason would be a little disappointed. Still, he never expected Jason to be this upset about it.

"Lee, do whatever it is you need to do and I'll talk with you later." James finished before he disconnected the call.
Lee stood with the phone still to her ear. She couldn't believe James refused to tell her that he would not date any other women. She felt completely heartbroken. James sat in his bedroom, stunned that Lee just broke up with him. He knew when Jason found out about them that it would be a strain on their relationship, but he never thought Lee would break up with him. James had been single for over ten years. He dated off and on but he never allowed himself to get serious with anyone for this reason and when he decided to put his fear of a broken heart on the back burner, he got his heart broken by his best friends Mom.
Weeks went by and Natalie was almost back to her normal self. She talked to her parents on a daily basis now and was getting ready to go back home to visit for a couple of days, Jason had agreed to go back with her to meet some of her friends. It had been almost seven years since she had been back home and she was looking forward to it, but what she doesn't know was that her mom and dad were throwing her a surprise party. Her mom had contacted all of Natalie's old friends from school and church. They almost all agreed to come and welcome her back to Indianapolis.

Chapter Forty

The Surprise

Jason and Lee's relationship was good since she agreed to stop seeing James, but the happiness and the spark that was there... was no longer there. Natalie felt bad for Lee. She felt that a mother should never have to choose between the man she loved and the child she loved. Natalie knew that Jason was old enough to understand.

"Jason, since we are leaving tomorrow, I want to sit down and talk with you about Lee and James."

"Natalie, I do not want to talk about that.

Her eyes narrowed. "I didn't ask you if you wanted to talk about that. You need to hear this from me. It's a shame that you can't accept the fact that your mom and one of your best friends have fallen in love. Why is it so hard for you to accept this? Don't you see how your mom is walking around here so sad? It hurts me to see Lee walking around here looking like she just lost her best friend. Is that how you want to see your mother?"

"She'll snap out of it soon," Jason shrugged.

"I can't believe you! You're acting so insensitive," Natalie said as she turned to face him. "When I was in the hospital what did you tell me? You told me that you wouldn't allow anyone to come between us because you never knew when God will call either one of us home. That should go for your mom as well. She deserves to be happy while she is still breathing, Jason. You better do right by her while she is here."

"Are you finished?"

Natalie just looked at Jason and rolled her eyes. "You are so damn stubborn." She responded with an aggravated sigh as she walked over to the cabinet to take a glass out. She went to the refrigerator and grabbed the carton of orange juice.

"Natalie turned back to look at Jason. "You know what? You're doing to Lee what my parents did to us. How did you feel when my dad forbade me from seeing you?"

"It didn't bother me not one bit because I knew I had you wrapped tightly around this big dick here." Jason grinned and started laughing as he ran out of the kitchen.

"That's right, you better run, talking out the side of your ass."

Meanwhile, Lee was busy trying to keep herself occupied. Jason no longer wanted her to cook and clean for them anymore. He had hired a housekeeper to come in four times a week to take care of everything that Lee use to do. Jason wanted his mom to enjoy the rest of her life and do whatever it was that made her happy, (except for being with James), but little did Jason know that his mom was planning to move out. She can no longer live under the same roof as Jason since she had to choose between Jason and James.
Natalie walked out of the kitchen and heads upstairs to Lee's room. She knocked softly on Lee's door.

"Come in."

Lee was just sitting on the end of her bed. Natalie's heart bled a little.

"Are you sure you won't come with us to Indianapolis for a couple of days? It'll do you some good to get away from this place. Besides, if you stay you know your son has asked John to come over and stay with you."

"That man won't give up, will he? What James and I should have done was to elope. What would Jason have done then? There wouldn't have been anything he could have done, but disown me."

"Don't worry, Lee. Your son will come around soon."

"Yeah, but it might be just too late."

"What do you mean?"

Lee smiled sadly. "When I broke it off with James I asked him to promise me that he wouldn't date anyone until I can work things out with Jason, but he refused to make me that promise."

"Oh, James is just hurt. I wouldn't worry about him dating anyone." Natalie said as she walked over and wrapped her arms around Lee.

"I love you so much and it hurts seeing you walk around here looking so sad."

"I love you, too. I love you as if you were my own blood."

James was at his home alone, thinking about Lee and Jason. Not only had he lost one of his best friends, but he lost the one person who made him feel whole again. James was a very handsome man; his rugged look turned many heads whenever he was around women of all ages, so finding a replacement wouldn't be hard... but no one could ever take Lee's place in his heart.

A couple of months ago, James was content living his life alone as a bachelor until he and Lee did the unthinkable, and now he knew that living his life alone was not what he wanted.

The next day Lee stood in the door and watched as Natalie and Jason head out for her parents in Indianapolis.

John was standing outside, watering the lawn. "John, I told you I could have done that."

"I know, but I wanted to make myself useful before I head over to the office to work on a case with James." Just as he said the name James he regretted it. He saw the look of hurt in Lee's eyes.

"Will you tell James I said hello since he won't take my calls?"

"I will just this one time. I don't want to get caught up in this and have Jason upset with me."

"I know. I appreciate you so much for not taking sides because I know you disagree with us."

"I don't disagree with you guys at all. I just knew how Jason would react I tried to stop you guys before the shit hit the fan."

Chapter Forty-One

The Party

Jason and Natalie arrived at her parents a little after six. Natalie was concerned as they pulled up because there were cars everywhere. The first thing that came to her mind was something had happened to one of her parents, but if that was the case, why hadn't anyone called her?

"Calm down Nat… I'm sure everything is fine." Jason said reassuringly as he exited the car, walking around to the passenger side and opening the door for her. They both walked back to the trunk to grab their overnight bags.

As the two walked up the stairs, the front door opened and Natalie's dad greeted the couple. Natalie's dad hugged her and kissed her on the cheek and then out of nowhere he embraced Jason. "I'm so glad to have you as my son-in–law," he whispered into Jason's ear.

Jason was thrown back for a minute. "I'm glad to hear that."

Just as the couple entered the home everyone yelled, "SURPRISE!" Natalie was knocked off her feet as she glanced into faces that she hadn't seen in a long time. Tears begin to form in her eyes, but she refused to let them fall.

Natalie turned and looked at her husband. "Did you know about this?"

"Yes, I'm afraid so." Jason smiled as Natalie nudged him in his rib.

Natalie introduced Jason to her longtime friends and to some of the church congregation. She was thrilled to have the opportunity to talk with her old friends and to catch up on the latest gossip and find out what's been going on in their lives.

That night, Natalie and her mom sat out on the front porch eating a piece of chocolate cake and drinking coffee.

"You know mom, I miss these days when you and I use to sit on the porch in the evenings and watch the neighborhood kids play out in the street. Nowadays kids don't even come out the house unless it's to go somewhere. They're too busy with the computer or those video games.

"I know. I remember when the streets were full of kids playing kickball or Dodgeball and racing up and down the street. "I swear I miss those days."

Natalie reached over and placed her hand on top of her mom's hand.

"Mom, I have missed you and dad so much."

"We feel the same way, baby," Mrs. Robinson said softly with tears in her eyes.

"It's hard for me to believe that we treated you and Jason the way we did. I hope the two of you truly forgive us."

"If we didn't mom, we would not be here right now."

Inside the Robinson's home, Jason and Mr. Robinson were enjoying a game of basketball on the Sports Channel. The finals were on and were between the Miami Heat and the Chicago Bulls.

"That Derrick Rose is something else," Mr. Robinson remarked.

"I know, he reminds me of a young Michael Jordan," Jason replied.

"Naw, he can't touch Michael, no one can… not even LeBron."

Minutes later Natalie and her mom entered the house. As Natalie walked in the room, she looked around. The living room looked a lot smaller than she imagined. The foyer was now painted an eggshell color instead of the sky-blue that she remembered. To the left still sat her dad's old recliner and the end-table. The light that used to sit there had now been replaced by a modern lamp.

Later that night, Jason and Natalie lay awake in bed talking. She was so glad that her parents made amends with her and her husband. She would have hated to have to attend one of their funerals without them ever accepting her husband and forgiving her for eloping.

Three days later, Lee was going out of her mind with boredom as she waited for Natalie and Jason to arrive home. Lee and John were sitting out back on the deck with John stretched out in one of the chairs, sleeping while the waterfall in the back that normally soothed Lee did nothing to heal her broken heart, so she got up and headed upstairs to her bedroom. She changed her clothes, grabbed her purse and keys and headed out.

Thirty minutes later, Lee pulled into James's driveway alongside a white Camry. She cut the engine, grabbed her purse and exited the car not once giving thought to the car parked in James's driveway. Lee made her way up the walkway to the front door and rang the doorbell. She waited and rang it again, but then she heard laughter coming from the backyard, so she heads in that direction. As Lee got closer, she could tell that one of the voices belonged to a woman. Lee continued to make her way through the gate to see James and a woman sitting out back having drinks. Lee was shocked. She could not believe what she was seeing. At first, she thought her eyes were playing tricks on her. Lee blinked a couple of times and then she proceeded to walk toward James. James sees a shadow from the corner of his eyes and turned around as Lee walked closer to him. James jumped to his feet. He never expected Lee to show up and now that he had a female guest who just happened to stop by, he can only imagine what was going through her mind.

The look on Lee's face said it all. The hurt, the sadness, and anger were all there.

"Lee, let me explain. It's not what you think."

"You go to hell, James," Lee bit out as she turned to leave so that James and his guest didn't see the tears that were threatening to fall. James ran after Lee leaving his guest behind. "Lee stop! Let me explain!"

"James, you don't have to explain anything to me. I understand we're no longer together and you didn't promise that you wouldn't see anyone while I worked on Jason so I understand." Lee was fighting back her tears as she got into her car. James could only stand and watch as Lee pulled off recklessly. He only hoped she made it home safe. The more he thought about her, the more he realized that he had to make Lee understand that there was nothing between him and his female guest.

James made his way back to his guest and explained things to her and told her that he had to leave. His female companion seemed a little irritated. She grabbed her purse and headed for her car without saying good bye.

James took the short cut to Jason's and arrived a little after Lee did. James found Lee still sitting in her car crying her heart out. James opened the car door and pulled Lee out and into his arms.

"I told you, sweetheart, it's not what you think. She stopped by uninvited. We were just having drinks. I promise that's all." James put his finger under Lee's chin and pushed her face upward until she was looking him in his eyes.

"Do you believe me?"

Unable to speak, Lee shook her head. James pulled her closer and pushed his way inside her mouth and kissed her like he had never kissed anyone in his lifetime. The two were so absorbed in each other that they never noticed Natalie and Jason as they pulled up in the driveway.

"What the fuck!" Jason growled as soon as he pulled up. He didn't even cut the engine off before hopping out and running toward James. Natalie yelled at Jason, which caused James and Lee to turn around. James turned around just in time to see Jason coming for him, but Jason was so swift he was upon James before James can move and threw a punch that hits him dead in his eye. The two begin throwing punches at each other until John came out and broke the fight up.

"I can't believe you two, acting like little kids! What the fuck is wrong with you guys?" John shouted as he walked back into the house to get his things together so he can head home.

Chapter Forty-Two

The aftermath

Several days go by and Natalie and Jason have not heard from Lee. She left with James right after their brawl. Natalie could tell that it had been bothering him that his mom had chosen James over him, but he had to realize that he was not a little boy anymore and that his mom had a life of her own to live.

Jason was standing at the back door looking out when Natalie walked up behind him and wrapped her arms around him. "Stop being so stubborn and give your mom and James a call. I guarantee you will feel a lot better."

Jason continued to stand there without saying a word. "Suit yourself," Natalie said as she turned to leave. Natalie went into the kitchen and took a seat on the ledge of the bay window and called Lee. Lee picked up on the third ring.

"Hello."

"Hey, it's Nat. How are you guys doing?"

"We're fine. How's that son of mines?"

"Stubborn as ever, but other than that he's okay."

"I wish he could see the damage he has done to James's eye. This is so ridiculous I'm so upset with him right now."

"I know, Lee. They've been friends for too long to let this happen. Jason won't even go into the office, he continues to work from home. I think he feels bad."

"Well, he should. I know he's hurt because James was like a brother to him, but he needs to realize that I can't help who I fall in love with any more than he can help that he fell in love with you, despite your parents forbid you from seeing him. He really needs to think about these things, because I won't choose between my son and James again because it is ridiculous."

It has been five days since Jason had been in the office. He had been working from home to avoid seeing James, but today he decided to go into the office after a phone call from one of the detectives working on Natalie's case. They told him they found the weapon used in

Natalie's stabbing, but the weapon was clear of any fingerprints, however, but the blood matched Natalie's DNA. Now, this brought them back to square one.

Furious, Jason hopped into his car and was headed for the office. As Jason drove he was hit with a ping of sadness. His wonderful life that he once knew had been turned upside down. It seemed every time he turned around, something new was going wrong. He wondered if he would he ever be able to get his life back to the way it used to be.

In the meantime, Natalie was headed to the grocery store to pick up some items for the Labor Day cookout. Jason doesn't know it, but she invited James and of course, Lee would be there. Natalie felt it was time for the two to kiss and make up. Life was too short to allow some bullshit to separate best friends.

Natalie pulled into the parking lot of Marsh grocery store unaware of her surroundings. She got out of the car, never giving thought to the white van that had pulled in beside her. As Natalie shut her car door, the side door of the white van opened and a man dressed in black from head to toe grabbed her and put a rag over her nose and mouth, causing her to pass out. It didn't take much for the man to get Natalie in his car because she never had time to even think about what was happening to her. It all happened too quickly. Afterwards, the man shut the side door and walked calmly around to the driver side of the van and hopped in taking off. This was done so smoothly that none of the customers in the parking ever suspected anything. In a second Natalie was taken away to Lord only knows where.

Jason pulled into the parking lot of the firm and the first car that he sees was James and beside his car was Lee's.

"I'll be damned," he said to himself as he punched the steering wheel. Jason continued to sit for a few more minutes before getting out of his car, but before he got out, John pulled up. Jason waited for John to get out before he got out.

"Look what the cat drug in," John said grinning a little.

Jason was in no mood for any of John's humor. "I see you got jokes, as usual."

John laughed. He knew Jason didn't want to see the two people already inside. John sees Jason's hesitation. "Come on, it won't be so bad." John nodded as he softly guided Jason up the sidewalk and through the front doors of the firm. As Jason entered the building, his heart was beating about 75mph, his hands were sweaty and his steps were slow. Just as he made it to his office, James office door opened and there stood James.

"Good afternoon." James said coolly.

"Yeah," Jason mumbled and nodded his head.

Lee followed James out the door behind him. She walked over and Jason gave her a hug and kissed her on her cheek. "How have you been and why haven't you called me?"

Jason ignored the question. "What are you doing here mom?"

"Well, if you would've taken the time to come into the office you would have known that James and John made a decision to hire a secretary," She said as she twirled around with her hands out to the side.

"What do you think?"

Jason couldn't help but laugh. "So you're a secretary now. I can't see you as anyone's secretary." Jason continued to laugh and shook his head.

"I beg your pardon. I have done damn well being their secretary and yours too. I have some skills, son. I have not always been your housekeeper. Who do you think kept the books for the Lorenz family?"

Jason looked at his mom with his mouth opened. He was shocked, to say the least. He had no idea that his mom worked for the Lorenz family.

"That's right, your mom worked for the drug family at one time. How do you think I met your father?" Lee said as she strolled down the hall to her desk in the receptionist area.

"I don't need to know anything else, mom!" Jason yelled after her. Jason took a seat behind his desk and picked up the phone to call John, "What's going on with the Ransom case?"

John smiled. "You'll have to ask James since he's the one handling that case now. I'm working on the Matthew case and boy I tell you, it's getting pretty deep. I may reach out to you and James for help. This family is off the chain. They continue to keep shit from me and time after time, I told them that I can't represent their sister right if they continue to keep secrets. I find out more and more each time we go to court. I'm at the end of the rope with these people. I am so ready to throw-in the towel with this bullshit case."

"That bad?'

"Hell yeah! They continue to feed me lies so how can I help them if they continue to do this?"

"Just be frank with them. Tell them if they don't come clean, they'll have to find someone else to represent them and be done with it."

"Yeah, but the sister is the one who they're hurting and they don't even realize it."

"John, you have to keep your feelings out of it."

Jason had that you've got to be kidding me look. Now he knows why he was still dealing with the family. He just hoped John knew what he was doing.

"Before you say anything, it's not what you think," John defended.

"What is it then?"

"I just want to do right by the sister. She's clearly being used by the family and so I want to help her as much as I can."

"Are you sure that's why?" Jason asked chuckling.

"Yes, the family is hanging her out to dry. I know she didn't commit the murder, I know one of the Matthew boys committed the crime and now is trying to put the blame on her because they believe the court will go easy on her, but little do they know, the court will make an example out of her because she's a prosecutor that has a family that is a crime family, but she doesn't see it that way neither does her family."

Later that day, James walked into Jason's office just as he was about to leave, "When you have some time, we need to sit down and talk."

"Yes we do," Jason responded stiffly as he walked past James and into the hallway. He looked back at James.

"Tell my mom to call me later."

James stood and watched as Jason walked out the building. "Man, I never knew he could be so damn stubborn."

Chapter Forty-Three

Abduction

Jason pulled into the driveway when he noticed Natalie's car was gone. He picked up his cell and dialed her number, and it went straight to voicemail.

"Hey babe, do you want to go out for dinner when you get home? Ring me back ASAP," Jason disconnected the call and got out heading up the walkway. Once inside, he headed straight for the shower. Today was a hard day for him, especially seeing James and his mom together.

"Will I ever get over this?" He seriously asked himself.
The hot water that ran down his body did little to help release the tension in his body. Just then he realizede Natalie hadn't returned his call. Jason cut the shower off, grabbed the towel and made his way to their bedroom where he grabbed a hold of his phone to check to see if he had missed any calls.
An hour goes by, then two, three and then five and still no word from Natalie. Something told Jason something was wrong. Jason phoned John and told him what he thought. John phoned James and they both head over to Jason's.

"Do you know what her plans were today?" John asked Jason.

"She was going to pick up some things from the grocery store for the cookout."

"What store was she going to?" James asked.

"I don't know, but I know she shops at Marsh Supermarket a lot of the times on East Washington Street."
John nods. "Let's go, let's take a ride over to Marsh then."

"Mom, can you stay here just in case she comes home or calls?"

"Yes, baby, I'll stay here. Don't worry... everything will be okay."

"I hope so," Jason forced a smile as he gave his mom a hug.
As the men were on their way to the Marsh Supermarket, there was an eerie feeling in the car. No one wanted to say anything but they all felt it. It took about twenty minutes for them to make it there, but

when they arrived, they saw her car parked in the parking lot, which told them all they needed to know.

As they moved closer to Natalie's car, Jason jumped out of the car before John had a chance to park. Jason ran over to the driver's side of the car and pulled on the handle. Natalie never had a chance to lock the door before she was attacked.

"Oh no…," Jason whispered. He yelled out, catching the security guards attention. The security guard walked over to where the men are standing. "Is everything okay?" He asked.

"The driver of this car has been missing since this afternoon. This is her husband and he's been calling her all afternoon and getting no response. Has anyone reported any activity out in the parking lot today?"

"No, but I just got here. We can check the surveillance camera if you like?"

The men followed the guard into the store and back to the main office. He explained the situation to the office manager on duty who was very eager to assist the men. They took a seat as the manager rewound the tape back and as sure as Jason felt something was wrong, it was proven in the video when they see a man dressed in all-black hop out of a white van abducting Natalie. The one good thing is that they were able to get a look at the license plate of the van.

James stepped out of the office and dialed Lee on the house phone and explained what has happened.

"Lee, I want you to lock up and don't open the door for anyone. Do you hear me?"

"James, you're scaring me."

"I intend to so you'll take this seriously. We don't know if this person has been watching Natalie at the house or not. If so, who's to say that he won't come back to the house for you?"

"For me… "there's a thick pause," James I am scared."

"Don't worry sweetheart, I'm on my way to get you."

James stepped back into the office. "I think we need to head home and call the boys in on this. I don't feel comfortable leaving Lee there by herself.

John hopped up, "I agree. Let's call the department from the house."

The three rode home in silence. Jason's mind was on Natalie while James thought about Lee and wondered how he would handle things if anything should happen to her. John, on the other hand, thought about Lori, the female prosecutor, he was trying to defend. True enough, he was getting too involved in this case because of his feelings for the attractive woman.

When they made it back to the house, Lee was nowhere to be found. Her car was still parked in the driveway so they figure she was somewhere close. James and Jason continued to search the house for her while John called their buddies on the police force.

When James and Jason can't find Lee, James decided to call her on her cell. He dialed her number and when it rang, they both turned in the direction of her room. The ringing of her cell phone was coming from her bedroom upstairs. Jason and James made their way upstairs to her bedroom. Jason slowly opened the door and sees her phone on the bedroom floor.

James's heart almost jumped out of his chest. He felt helpless and scared that they may not see Lee alive again.

"Oh my God," Jason gasped. "This can't be happening. This has got to be a bad dream," he almost whispered.

Jason dropped onto Lee's bed and began to cry. He sees his world coming to an end. Natalie had disappeared and now his mom is gone as well. The two people that he loved more than life, "Who would do this?" he questioned as he looked up at James.

"I don't know, but if they lay one hand on Lee, I will kill them with my bare hands," James growled darkly as he headed downstairs. Several hours later, James heard a knock at the door. James rushed to answer and to his surprise there stood Lee bloody and beaten.

"Shit!" he almost screamed and then he yelled for Jason and John. As soon as Lee realized she was in the arms of James she told him who did this to her.

"I am going to kill his ass… just wait." James grumbled with so much anger in his voice that his body shook from the timbre. Jason was beside himself. He now knew the person who had Natalie, but where?

Lee passed out so they call the paramedics and followed them as they transported her to the hospital. Jason paced back and forth in the waiting room while Lee had surgery on her jaw. Jason couldn't wait until he was able to talk with his mom. He only hoped she could tell him where Natalie was. When the doctor came out to talk with the men, they learned that Lee's jaw had been broken in three places and that she suffered some cuts and bruises to her face and both eyes. He intentionally left out the part about her being raped. When the doctor asked Lee earlier if she had been raped, she nodded her head yes while tears rolled down her face.

She was able to get out "don't tell" so the doctor decided to let Lee tell them about the rape.

"Lee is one lucky lady. I can't believe she was returned. This sounds like someone trying to send a message to someone if you ask me." The doctor said to the men. "I had to wire her mouth shut so her jaw will heal correctly, so that means she is not to talk.

I left a writing pad and pen by her bedside, though. I've given her a sedative for the pain so she will be out for a while, so if I were you, I would go home and get some rest. We will take good care of her."

Chapter Forty-Four

The truth revealed

Jason and John went home to wait on a few colleagues to stop by while James made himself comfortable in Lee's hospital room. He was not going to leave her alone anymore, he didn't know what this person was up to and what if he tried to do something to her again? No… he will be ready for him this time.

James woke to the sound of the door shutting. He jumped up and rushed to Lee's side making sure she was okay. He didn't know that while he slept the nurses have been in and out of Lee's room all night checking on her.

When Lee finally awoke, she tried to smile, but the pain that shot to her jaw was unbearable. The tears that she cannot hold back slowly rolled down her face.

"Don't try to talk sweetheart," James told her as he walked over to her and wiped the tears away with his finger before handing her the notepad and pen.

"The nurse left this notepad and pen for you to use to communicate with instead of you trying to talk.

Your jaw's been wired to help improve your stability. It'll remain wired for at least six to eight weeks, so guess what? It is soft foods for you young lady." Lee eyes almost pop out and James laughed.

"It won't be that bad. Do you need more pain medication?" James asked as he sees the pain in her face.

Lee nodded her head yes. Lee began to write on the notepad and turned to look at James.

"I don't have time for this bullshit." Lee wrote.

James laughed at her. "You are something else woman, but that's why I love you." He smiled and kissed her on the lips.

Lee wrote:

"Don't do that. You're turning me on looking at me like that and kissing me. James I'm so glad to see you. I thought I would never see you again… I am so glad I was dropped off or should I say

214

thrown out of the white van a block down from the house. After I got off the phone with you, I went around to make sure every window and door was locked when I heard something on the deck. It sounded like glass breaking so I went to check it out. As I stepped out onto the deck, I saw a big jar that had dropped on the deck so I went back inside to get the broom and dustpan to clean up the mess. When I returned, there was a man dressed in black with a gun in his hand pointed at me. He walked toward me and that was the last thing I remembered before waking in an empty building."

James read all of this and sighed. "Lee, I hate to ask you this, but I have to and I want you to be honest with me. Did Derrick rape you?" The scared look on Lee's face told James what he needed to know. James wiped his eyes with his fingers as he tried to digest this bit of information. Lee was terrified that he would never want to touch her again. She looked into his eyes so soft and sympathetic then broke down crying making sad chuffing noises through the wiring running through her poor mouth.

"Hey, hey…" James leaned over and hugged her gently. She clung to him as if he was a life preserver and she was in the middle of the ocean.
Seeing Lee in this condition made James angrier than ever. He walked out of Lee's room to avoid her seeing him shed his own tears, but Lee took this as he didn't want to be with her anymore since another man had taken her.
Lee began to write on her pad again as the tears flow as she waited for James to come back to her room.

"James I am sorry that he raped me, please forgive me and please whatever you do, don't tell Jason, please I beg you.
 I will try to understand if you don't want to have anything else to do with me, but I thought I meant more to you than that. Derrick did this to me to get back at Jason. I believe he has Natalie."

As Lee finished writing, the nurse came in with some medication to help relieve some of the pain she was feeling. Lee tried her best to stay awake and wait for James to return, but she lost the battle and was quickly asleep. When James returned, he saw her message and rushed to call Jason, but before he left, he made sure that the message was destroyed.

Twenty minutes later, Jason and John arrived at the hospital and waited in Lee's room for her to awake. An hour later, Lee opened her eyes to a room full of handsome men. At first, she thought she died and went to heaven until she laid eyes on her son.

"Hey mom, how are you feeling?" Jason asked as he kissed her on the forehead. "Mom, can you tell us where Derrick took you?"
Lee looked around for her writing pad and pen. James walked up and handed it to her. She looked at his face to see if there was any resentment in his eyes, but James avoided eye contact with her. She also noticed that her message from earlier was no longer on the pad she was thankful for that.

"Jason, I wish I could tell you where I was, but the only thing I can tell you is that it was a large vacant warehouse.
I know it wasn't too far from the house because it didn't take any time getting back to the house. I thought I heard Natalie voice telling him not to hurt me. I believe she was tied up as well because she kept begging him to let her go to the restroom."

"Okay, we need to check all vacant warehouses near my house and see what we find. I know off hand of about four vacant warehouses. Why don't we split up and check them out and meet back here in an hour. "Jason kissed Lee's forehead. "Mom, I want you to get some rest. We'll be back later. I love you mom and I'm so sorry this happened to you."
James felt bad and ashamed of his actions earlier so he didn't even look at her before leaving which broke her heart.
Lee held the tears that were threatening to fall until the men left the room and then she let loose. Her heart was breaking and for what all because Derrick's slimy ass raped her. She noticed how James avoided eye contact with her and how he stayed in the back of the room.
How can a man that claimed to love me treat me this way at a time like this? She questioned herself.

"James, why are you so quiet?" Jason asked. "And why didn't you say anything to my mom before we left?"
"I have my reasons."

"Well, this isn't the time to act distant. If you really want to be in her life, now's the time to show it or should I say show me, if not, leave her alone. I won't stand by and let you hurt her any more than she's already been hurt."

"Man, I ain't in no mood to hear that shit right now."
Jason and John stopped dead in their tracks and looked at James like he had lost his damn mind. They knew something was up now because this was not James. Jason walked up to James and grabbed him by the collar. "What do you mean you ain't in no mood to hear this shit?' Nigga, this is my mom that we're talking about not some bitch out here on the fuckin street."
John got in between the two men. "Hey, this is neither the time nor the place for this. James, you are sounding pretty foul right now. What's up with you?"
James jerked away from Jason. "That mother-fucker raped her," He said as he let the tears fall. There was a stunned silence, then Jason spoke "Oh hell no… not my mom. That mother fucker better hope I never catch his ass because I promise on my dad's grave I will kill him." Jason turned suddenly and hit the wall with his fist. James walked off and left the men behind. He needed air and to be alone to clear his mind. He was not sure if he can get over the fact that Derrick raped Lee.

"How can I be with her now that she was raped by this son of a bitch?" He asked himself.

"John I'll catch up with you later," Jason said as he headed back to his mom's room.
Jason entered the room, eyes red from the tears that he had shedded for her. One look at him and Lee knew James had told her secret. "I am sorry mom, I am so sorry he did this to you. I swear I will find him and make him pay." He walked over and sat down beside her bed and laid his head on her stomach.
Lee was unable to speak, but shed more tears as she laid her hand on her son's head. She couldn't believe her life had turned out like this. She knew Derrick despised her, still she never thought he would do something like this to her. She hoped the men caught him and beat him to death. She would never feel safe again as long as she knew he was still out there somewhere. Her heart ached for Natalie because there was no telling what he had done to her. Lee could only hope she was still alive and well and that the men found her in time.

John reached the location of one of the vacant warehouses and as he approached the entry way some young boys call out to him.

"Hey, are you with the guy that had those two women here?" John walked over to the young boys. "What guy and what women?"

"There was this really ugly looking guy here with two women. He had them tied up, but we only saw him leaving with one of the women."

"And when was this?"

"He left about an hour ago with one of the women."

"And you guys didn't call the police?"

"It ain't none of our business." The younger boy said defensively.

"Any time you see someone doing something wrong, it should always be your business. We have to look after our own, especially our women. Do you guys understand?"
The other boy shook his head, "I told you we should have called the cops."

"Can you guys do me a favor? If you should see this guy come back can you give me a call?" John handed the older boy his business card.
John continued his walk into the building and up to the third floor where he sees ropes, blankets, and empty water bottles.
John pulled out his cell and dialed Jason. "Hey Jason, I'm at the Jameson building and from what I'm being told by some young boys, I just missed Derrick about an hour ago. They said they saw him leave with a woman, which I suspect is Natalie."

"Damn, lord knows where he could be now." "Thanks, John I'll see you at the house soon," Jason said and hung up.
John sent James a text telling him about what he found out and asking him to meet them at the house.
James was in his own world. He didn't meet up with the guys like he was supposed to and continued to ignore their phone calls and texts. He was just not in the mood to be around anyone and he wished he could forget about Lee being raped by Derrick, but he couldn't and didn't know if he will ever look at her the same way again. He knew this was not her fault, but he simply cannot bring himself to accept this and move on with her. James continued to sit in his car parked in his driveway with a bottle of Hennessey. He wanted more than anything to drown his sorrows away in his bottle.

Chapter Forty-Five

Guilt

Two weeks later

James woke to the sound of loud banging at his front door. He laid there for a minute or two hoping whoever it was would leave, but the banging continued.

"Dammit, who is it?" James yelled at the door.

"Open the damn door man!" John shouted.

James wearily got off the couch and swung the door open.

"What is so important that you're about to tear my damn door down?"

"Are you serious man?" The woman that you claim to love is lying at home crying her eyes out because she believes you don't love her anymore-- and besides that, Jason is ready to come over here and beat the hell out of you and guess what, I wish he would. You've got some nerve treating Lee like this. I tried to stay out of y'all mess, but right now, if you say one wrong word, I'm liable to beat your ass myself. James, you're better than this or at least I thought you were. Why are you doing this to Lee?"

James threw his hands up in the air and walked over to his loveseat and sat down. He rubbed his hand over his face.

"I know I'm wrong, but I can't get up enough nerves to face her right now. I can't get over the fact that another man had her. I know I'm wrong for this… but I can't do it right now."

"Man, all you have to do is explain this to Lee and that this is going to take some time for you to get over. You don't just leave the woman you love hanging and wondering about how you feel about her. You've just given Jason all the reason in the world to demand that you stay away from her."

"Man, I feel so bad right now, but I can't face her like this!" James cried out as tears started to roll down his face. "I know she didn't ask for any of this, but to know that Derrick's nasty- ass fucked my woman…" James shook his head.

"It's just too much for me right now."

"How do you think it makes her feel? Jason said she constantly has nightmares now. He's really worried about her. He's thinking about taking her to see a shrink."

"Are you serious?"

"Yes… and you're not making matters better. I think she would feel a lot better and safer if you were there."

"Oh my God, I am feeling really bad right now. I can't imagine what Lee and Jason think about me or how they'll react if I show up now. How can I possibly make this up to them?"

"I don't know, but what I do know is if you care about Lee the way you say you do, you'd better do something fast or I am afraid you will lose Lee altogether."

James' heart ached as he listened to what John was saying. He knew John was telling him the truth, but he didn't want to hear it right at this moment. He wanted to continue having his pity party. Poor James!

"Well, I've told you what you need to know. Now it's up to you to do the right thing or lose Lee forever." John finished as he got up to leave.

A couple weeks went by and James had just now gotten enough nerves to go visit Lee. He didn't know how all this was going to turn out--- especially with Jason---, but he had to try to do whatever he could to make things right with Lee. He now knows he cannot live without her.

Jason sat at the kitchen table trying to get his self together. He was hoping and praying that he would find Natalie, yet each day that went by, his faith continued to vanish slowly. Jason continued to sit when he heard a knock at the door. Thinking it could be Natalie, he rushed to the front door to find James standing there with flowers and a card for Lee.

"What the hell do you want?"

"Jason, I am so sorry for the way I have been acting lately. I came over here to speak to you and then Lee. I know I owe you guys the biggest apology. Just hear me out."

Jason moved out of the way and allowed James to enter. Jason heads for the kitchen as James shut the door behind him and followed Jason into the kitchen. James pulled a chair out across from Jason as he sat the flowers and card on the table.

"I know there is no excuse for my behavior, but I couldn't get over the fact that Derrick raped Lee. I tried so hard to get over it, but it tore me up inside. I didn't think about anyone else's feelings but my own and that was so selfish of me. It didn't dawn on me how I was making Lee and you feel until John talked some sense into me a couple of weeks ago. I just got up enough nerves to come over here not knowing if you would punch my lights out or not. I hope you'll accept my apology for staying away and not being here for you and Lee."

Jason looked up at James, "I don't know what to say. When this all happened to my mom I was ready to forgive you and accept your relationship, but now I don't know what to think. James, I've known you for a very long time and I thought I knew what type of person you were. Not once did I ever think you would run out on my mom when she needed you but you did. So now I'm supposed to just forget all that has happened and allow you back into our lives? I'm not sure I can do that. My mom might, but right now I don't know if I can."

James nodded. "Jason I truly understand. I just want you to know that I never meant to hurt Lee or you by any means and that's why I'm here, and to find out if Lee will allow me to be a part of her life again, I will do whatever it takes to prove to you and Lee that I love her more than anything and that she will never have to worry about me running out on her ever again. On another note, has there been any word on Natalie's whereabouts?"

Jason shook his head. "No, I sit here every evening waiting for her to walk through those doors and each day, I lose more and more hope that I'll ever see her again. I believe Derrick has her and if I know him, he has left the country with her and if that's the case he'll kill her before he would risk her coming back to me."

"Man, I'm so sorry," James said as he walked over and patted Jason on the back. "I know she means the world to you. That's one of the reasons I came over here. Natalie is a reality- check. I don't ever want to lose Lee, not now… or ever."

"Can I go up and see her?"

"Sure, but don't get her upset and remember she can't talk Doctor's orders."

James smiled as he headed upstairs. He was thankful that he still had an opportunity to talk and be with Lee if she would have him.

Chapter Forty-Six

Now or never

As James climbed the stairs, he thought about what he was going to say to Lee. He decided to just be honest with her about how he was feeling and now how he knows he was being selfish.

James stood at Lee's door, unsure of how things would go and he only hoped she was a forgiving woman. James knocked lightly on the door twice before Lee opened the door. Lee was expecting to see Jason, but instead she was so surprised when she sees James standing there with flowers that she had to do a double take and stepped back. James puts a finger to his lips. "Don't try and say anything, let me do all the talking." James walked into the room and handed Lee the flowers and card. Seeing that her mouth was still wired shut, he walked over to the table and looked for a notepad and pen. "Have a seat, please." He told her as he handed her the notepad and pen.

"I know I was wrong for staying away as long as I have and I deserve any treatment that you give me. I just ask that you hear me out and be more considerate than I've been." James sighed and launched. "Lee, when I found out that Derrick had raped you, it did something to me inside. To know that the woman I love had been touched by such a scum was just a little too much for me to bear. I was angry and then I got upset at you for telling me. Now I realize I had no reason to act that way toward you; it wasn't as if you asked to be raped especially not by Derrick. At one point I didn't believe I could even be with you anymore, but now I know I was just thinking about myself and that was wrong. I ask you to please forgive me because I had no reason to act like that. I was being a jerk and if you can't forgive me, I truly understand and I deserve whatever decision you make."

Lee looked at James with tears in her eyes. Her heart ached for weeks for him and he was nowhere in sight. He wouldn't answer John or Jason's phone calls. She continued to think about what James had just said and thought about how he had hurt her. Lee began to write down her feelings on the notepad and handed it over to James.

"James you have hurt me very much, much more than what Derrick has done to me. Out of all people, I never imagine that you would act as you have done. If you would have ask me two weeks ago, if I could forgive you, I might have said yes, but right now, I don't know if I can ever forgive you. The day you walked out on me is when I needed you more than anything and you were not there. How can I forgive a man who claimed to love me as much as you have confessed to me? I just don't know how I can forgive you. Right now I can't, but that doesn't mean that in the future I may have a change of heart and forgive you. I will need some time."

James was heartbroken, but he understood what he had done was cruel. He would wait as long as it took for Lee to change her mind. "I understand Lee and trust me, I don't blame you not one bit, but I do want you to know that I will wait for you as long as it takes because you are my world and without you, my life is incomplete." James bent down and kissed Lee on her forehead.

"You take care of yourself, and if you need anything, just have Jason give me a call and I'll come running. I love you, Lee."

Lee sat with tears threatening to fall as James walked out. She wondered if she had done the right thing by letting him go because she remembered the last time and what happened when she showed up unannounced and found him in the backyard with a female guest. Lee walked over to the window to get a glimpse of James as he walked to his car and at that moment she realized that no matter - what he had done to her, she loved him and wanted to spend the rest of her life with him.

Knowing that she would not make it outside in time to stop James, she ran downstairs to Jason with her notepad and tears in her eyes.

"Mom, what's wrong?" Jason asked, immediately concerned. She wrote quickly, Jason please call James to come back. I need him in my life."

Seeing the hurt and sadness in his mom's eyes, he was willing to do whatever it would take to make her happy so he pulled out his cell phone and call James.

No sooner than Jason hung up with James he was at their front door knocking. Jason opened the door and stepped out of James' way as he rushed to Lee. Jason had to say that seeing his mom happy pulled at his heart. He only wished Natalie were here. Every single day that went by, it seemed as though he missed her more and more.
Jason grabbed his coat and his keys and headed out to search for Natalie. He had done this every evening since her disappearance. He went back to the warehouse and searched for any clues that he may have missed the last four weeks… something; anything. Jason's heart would not allow him to give up hope of not ever seeing her again. He would move mountains to get her back.

Several months have gone by and still no word on Natalie. The one good thing was that Lee was back to her old self. Her jaw had healed perfectly and she and James were engaged. Lee had been planning a Christmas wedding, but at times, her heart ached for Natalie and Jason. Sometimes she felt bad for being so in love with James while her son hurts so much for his wife.
John, on the other hand, won his court case and proved that Lori did not commit the crime she was being framed for. Her oldest brother had set her up and figured that since she was a prosecutor, the court would go easy on her. Lori and John began seeing each other on a regular basis.

Thanksgiving Day

Jason opened up his home for Thanksgiving to his family and friends. Lee and Lori agreed to do the cooking for everyone.
Lee and Lori were busy in the kitchen making the meal. "Lee, how long have you known James?"
"Honey, I've known James for years. James and Jason have been friends for over twenty years, but I didn't really notice James until about six years ago and I tried to hide my feelings, but one day I saw how he looked at me and he noticed how I looked at him and we went for it, not knowing how we would feel but as it turned out, we both felt the same way. So here we are, engaged to be married in less than a month."
Lee had a huge smile on her face. "Oh my God, that is so sweet."

"Yeah, I have to admit that I felt as though I would never find anyone and fall in love, but I guess if you're patient God will send you the perfect mate in due time."

"Tell me about John. I assume you have known him for just as long?" Have you met many of his women friends?"

"To be honest, you're the first person that I've actually met." I know he's dated many women, but he's never brought them around. So if I were you, I would consider myself lucky."

Lori smiled at that. She liked Lee and was happy that Lee and James had found happiness with each other and that Jason had finally come around and accepted their relationship.

As the family, John, James and their police buddies sat around the table, Jason realized how blessed he was, even if he didn't have his wife here with him. Jason began to say grace, but got choked up and James finished where Jason left off.

"Thanks, James... or should I say, dad?" Everyone at the table laughed.

Later that night, James and Lee headed over to his place. James grinned slyly. "I hope you packed us some sweets because when I get finished with you I'm gonna want something else sweet to eat."

"James, you are so bad and to think I almost gave up on you."

"Baby, you could never give up on me. I knew you were hooked a long time ago even before I laid this pipe down."

"What are you talking about?"

"Remember at my twenty- fifth birthday party at your house when you walked in on me in the restroom with my Jimmie out? I knew you wanted me then. I started to say something to you then, but I didn't because of Jason and how young he was. I told myself then I would wait until I felt he was old enough to handle me dating his mom."

Lee made a puff sound and waved her hand. "You are so fucking full of yourself. I did not want you."

"Yeah?" Is that why I had to push you out of the bathroom? You were ready to jump all on this big dick."

Lee laughed. You are something else. I can't believe you. If you thought I wanted to jump on your dick why did you push me out of the bathroom?"

"Did you forget your husband was in the next room?"

"Oh, I forgot all about that."

"I know. Once you saw the D you forgot about everything."
Lee shoved James out of the way. "Get out with that big head of
yours."

"You love this big head don't you?"

"Whatever!"
James walked up behind Lee and pulled up her dress and tore her
panties off. He spread her legs as he eased down until he was on his
knees. He spreads her butt cheeks apart and begins to slide his tongue
from the front to the back of her ass. Lee held onto the counter as the
feeling of his wet thick tongue slid over her clit.

"Oh, James baby, this feels so damn good." Lee turned her body
around and hopped on the counter, opening her legs wide so James
can have better access to her pussy as her juices sipped out."

"Whose pussy is it?"

"It's yours, baby, this pussy belongs to you and you only."

Chapter Forty-Seven

A new beginning

James and Lee tied the knot on Christmas Eve and quickly afterwards they took off for their honeymoon to Jamaica. The first couple of days the newlyweds stayed in bed, but on the third day, they decided to get out and enjoy the island.

"Come on James it's time to see the island babe."

"All I want to do is see you."

"Love, you have the rest of your life to see me and why are you so damn horny?"

"Shit, that ass turns me on. Every time you walk by me it gets hard."

"Stop lying and get your ass in the shower. Meet me downstairs in thirty minutes are I'll leave without you. I'll have one of those Jamaican men show me around."

"Like hell, you will."

Thirty minutes later, James made his way to the lobby of the hotel.

"So babe, what is it that you want to do?"

"I want to go shopping and later I want to go on the dinner cruise."

"Okay, let's do this." James nodded in agreement.

As they rode into town, Lee noticed a woman who looked a lot like Natalie. "It couldn't be." She breathed.

"What are you talking about babe?"

"I thought I saw Natalie."

"What!"

"Yeah, I thought I saw Natalie. The lady looked so much like Natalie that it scared me."

"Where did you see her?"

"Back there at the little coffee shop."

"Hey sir, can we get off here? Thanks"

When Lee and James got off the shuttle bus they headed back to the little coffee shop. "This is where you thought you saw her?"

"Yes."

James noticed how some of the men in the coffee shop were looking at them, which caused the hairs on the back of his neck to stand up. James grabbed a hold of Lee's arm and guided her to the next shop.

"Did you see how they looked at us?"

"Yeah, what's up with that?"

"Well, I have a funny feeling that you did see Natalie. Derrick is from Jamaica. It would make sense for him to bring her here to keep her away from Jason. I want to call Jason, but I don't want to get his hopes up. We need to get back to the hotel. I need to get in touch with a buddy of mine that has some family here and see if I can get them to help me find Natalie or the person who looked like her before calling Jason. I 'm sorry sweetie, I know you wanted to get some shopping done today, but I can have someone at the hotel escort you while I handle business."

"Are you crazy? I don't want to go anywhere without you just in case Derrick is here. I don't trust him. What if he saw us and tries to take me again?"

James sees the look of fear in Lee's eyes. "Don't worry sweetheart, I won't let you out of my sight. You'll be safe with me." James was in thought for a moment. Since you are Jason's mom, do you think I should call him now or wait?'

"He needs to know now, James. I wish you would have told me Derrick was from here I would have picked another place for us to have our honeymoon."

"Baby, don't let that thought keep you from enjoying our trip. When they arrived back at the hotel, Lee sat out on the balcony as James phoned Jason then he phoned his buddy.

"Hey, I'm going to make this up to you... okay?"

"You promise?"

"I promise, sweetie. So what do you want to do while we wait for James and John to arrive?"

"So they're coming."

"Yes, Jason knows, this may or may not be Natalie but he said he has to know and John wants to come. I think he's bringing Lori."

"Oh, I hope so. Let's get something to eat and decide on something to do until they get here."

The next day John, Jason, and Lori arrived. Lee was so glad that Lori was able to come. Now she would have someone to keep her company while the men worked, but she did not plan on being too far from them just because of Derrick. James's buddy confirmed with his relatives that Derrick was here and had a female companion that fits the description of Natalie. His friend's brother was on his way over to take them around to see if they can find out where Derrick was hiding out.

Lee and Lori were sitting in the lobby as the men approached.

"Hey, why don't you ladies go shopping while we handle business?"

Lee's guard went up. "Can John come with us as our body guard?"

"Lee doesn't feel comfortable being away from me while Derrick is running loose around here," James told the men.

"Of course, darling, I'll be your bodyguard." John nodded.

"John you are so sweet," Lee said as Lori smiled in return.

John, Lee and Lori head into town for some shopping. "John, that's where I thought I saw Natalie, at that little coffee shop."

John eyed it. "I believe Derrick's family owns that shop. I do remember him telling me about a coffee shop that his family owned over here called the Rituals Coffee House. Can we get off here and stop in there?"

"John I want to shop."

"I promise you can go shopping afterward."

"Okay, only if you promise shopping afterward."

As the three get off the shuttle and head toward the coffee shop, Lori hugged Lee. "I know this has not been the honeymoon, you imagined."

"No, it hasn't, but my hubby is going to make it up to me later."

"Oh my God!" Lee whispered loudly.

"What's wrong?"

"The hairs on the back of my neck just stood straight up. I feel like someone is watching me. I need my hubby," Lee said as fear set in. Lee pulled out her phone and dialed James' number.

"Babe where are you? I am so scared, I feel as though someone is watching me."

James laughed. Don't worry It's just your man watching you and the way that ass is moving."

"James, this is not the time for jokes. I am serious… I'm scared."

"Babe, I am right across the street watching you guys in the coffee shop. I need for you guys to leave and do some shopping. Tell John we got this."

"Okay, babe. . . I'm so relieved."

Lee walked over and whispered in John's ear. John turned around and sees his buddies. "Okay, let's go shopping, ladies."

As the three head out of the coffee shop, an older man bum-rushed Lee and grabbed her purse. It was a good thing that John was with them because John knocked the man to the ground and placed his foot on the man's throat.

"Lee, get your purse. How in the fuck can you treat a lady like this you piece of shit?" John yelled at the guy as James, Jason, and Ralph ran across the street to the incident.

"I'm sorry, I was paid to snatch her purse."

"Who paid you?" James demanded as he grabbed the guy up by his collar and threw him against the concrete wall.

"His name is Derrick Snow."

"That's it, ladies, back to the hotel," James demanded.

Back at the hotel, the men agreed that it would best for the ladies to head back to the states so they could do what they needed to do without having to worry about their safety.

"No! This is my honeymoon and I am not leaving without you!"

"Mom, stop being stubborn and listen to me and your husband."

Lee looked at Jason like he had three heads. "It's always something to keep me from James and I'm tired of it."

James stepped in, "Babe look, once we are finished here, I promise we'll take our honeymoon for two weeks anywhere you want to go." James walked over to Lee and grabbed her by the waist and brought her close to him and kissed her hard. "I can't do my job here and keep you safe."

The next morning Lee and Lori boarded a plane back to the states. The ladies were sad, but they know it was best for them to leave and let their men take care of business.

The men stay in Jamaica another week, but were unable to locate Derrick. So they decided to come back to the States and wait for about a month or so and go back. They wanted to return when Derrick least expected them.

In the meantime, James and Lee had their honeymoon in Paris. The two newlyweds had the best time of their life and had plans of returning in the near future.

The End

About the author

Denise Hill was raised in Indianapolis, Indiana, where she resides today with her son Daniel and her daughter Devin. Denise worked at one of the largest financial institution in Indianapolis as a Sales & Marketing Associates for 27 ½ years. Today she works for herself at DH Publishing & Production Company, where she plans to turn her books into movies. Denise graduated from Thomas Carr Howe High School and received her Business degree from the University of Phoenix. Denise has always enjoyed writing and published her first novel in April 2014. This is her second novel and she is currently working on other novels and a movie.

Double Crossed II coming 2016

Scandalous 2016

Because He Loved Me 2019

Envy 2017

Torn 2018

Love of a Lifetime 2014- Movie

The House Guest 2018-Movie